MURDER AND THE SCENT OF NUTMEG

A POSIE PARKER MYSTERY #16

L. B. HATHAWAY

WHITEHAVEN

WHITEHAVEN MAN PRESS

First published in Great Britain in 2024
by Whitehaven Man Press

(http://www.lbhathaway.com, email:
permissions@lbhathaway.com)

A CIP catalogue record for this book is
available from the British Library.

ISBN (e-book:) 978-1-913531-35-5
ISBN (paperback:) 978-1-913531-36-2

For the Posie fans, with so many thanks.

Also by L.B. Hathaway

The Posie Parker Mystery Series

1. Murder Offstage
2. The Tomb of the Honey Bee
3. Murder at Maypole Manor
4. The Vanishing of Dr Winter
5. Murder of a Movie Star

(The stand-alone novella, A Christmas Case)

6. Murder in Venice
7. The Saltwater Murder
8. Murder on the White Cliffs
9. Marriage is Murder?
10. Murder in the London Lights
11. Murder in Tuscany
12. Murder in a Chelsea Garden
13. Murder and the Mermaid
14. Murder through the Mirror
15. Murder on the Night Train to Paris
16. Murder and the Scent of Nutmeg
17. Murder and the Queen's Jewels
18. Murder in the Mountains

... and more to come.

PART ONE
Temple Church, London
(February 12, 1926)

One

When bad things happen, often we look to the past for comfort, for security.

So it was now for Posie Parker.

She sat in a dark pew of the Temple Church, London; a place that ached of her childhood, of other, starrier times.

Arguably she was London's premier female Private Detective, and she should have been on top of her game, but she had a bunch of problems.

The year had started badly, and she'd taken a bit of a knocking.

An eventful trip to Paris in January had caused her to do some soul-searching upon her return, and, truth be told, she hadn't felt much like work. Hadn't felt much like anything, really. There was a matter needing her attention in Switzerland, which should have been exciting, but Posie couldn't summon up the enthusiasm to sort it out, and the papers which related to it sat on her desk at work, in a neglected little pile.

At the moment everything felt wrong, even her marriage to a man who was undeniably on top of *his* game: Richard Lovelace, the most senior policeman in the land, Chief Commissioner of New Scotland Yard.

Richard Lovelace was English to the core, and his

signature scent - Penhaligon's trusty 'Blenheim Bouquet' - encapsulated this. He was unutterably sexy, kind, older than Posie, and she loved him within an inch of her life, but there had certainly been something on his mind lately, too, and it hadn't been his wife.

In two days' time it was Valentine's Day. Today was the last working day before it, but Posie expected Richard had forgotten all about it, and she doubted that there was a gift or surprise on the horizon for her.

She'd thought she'd give him a 'reminder' before breakfast this morning. She'd dressed provocatively, in scarlet suspenders and a red feather boa, and nothing much else, and kissed him awake.

But she'd been rebuffed: Richard had jumped out of bed in a tearing hurry and hared out of the flat at breakneck speed for work, barely bothering to wish her goodbye; not even staying long enough to eat his porridge.

Grumpily, and bloody-mindedly, Posie had then ripped off the suspenders and dressed herself up to the nines in clothes more suited to a party, all with a decidedly silver tinge.

She'd show him.

Still, she was worried.

These last couple of days Posie could have sworn she'd smelt another woman's perfume about Richard; a decidedly cheap amber-ish musk lingering cloyingly on his skin. It was a young scent, and tawdry: worlds away from the sweet fresh bloom of the Parma Violet which Posie herself favoured and had worn ever since she was eighteen.

But she doubted herself, too. Doubted her senses. She'd been feeling decidedly off colour and achy these last few days. A cold? Something the children had passed to her?

And what was she supposed to do now with Richard, anyhow? Wait for the lipstick on his collar? Jazz herself up even more? Ask him about it directly?

Have you found someone else?

Who is she? Tell me.

She'd sound pathetic, desperate. No, that wasn't the way she worked.

Work.

Posie sighed.

Real work, her own little Detective Agency at Grape Street, near Shaftesbury Avenue, usually a safe haven in any kind of crisis, was complicated too.

Three weeks ago Posie had engaged a new friend, the very lovely but eminently work-shy Suzannah Scotland, as a temporary secretary, and the arrangement was already panning out badly for all concerned.

Sunny but disorganised, Suzannah had no concept of time at all and 'URGENT' packages had been left unsent, with disastrous results, and bills had been left unpaid, with most incoming mail lying around, unopened, as if waiting for better weather.

The office was a nasty mess of overflowing ashtrays and long-dead flowers in greasy vases, and there were grimy cups and saucers piled up all about the place.

Worse, Suzannah seemed to view the office telephone apparatus as being for her very own personal recreation, which was, at present, attempting to keep the rather dashing Sergeant James Fox of Scotland Yard intrigued enough to woo her, which was all to the good, but the last half-monthly telephone bill had been astronomical.

Len, Posie's erstwhile partner at the agency, was livid with Posie for having installed someone so hopeless at the task, and every time Posie crossed the threshold of the office, she felt her heart sink at the prospect of either sacking Suzannah, or arguing with a very ratty Len, or both, and so she avoided them.

Coward that she was.

Posie either kept to her tiny back office, or else, as was happening more and more, she didn't linger.

She'd dash in, grab her files, any new post she could get her hands on, and run.

Like today.

She went into the Detective Agency at mid-morning, dressed in her silvery best, relieved to find it empty.

Then she hurried out, cutting along to the Lyons Cornerhouse on the Strand to read her small pile of post in peace, but the place was festooned with glitteringly pink premature 'VALENTINE'S DAY' banners, and simperingly love-sick lovers were perched at every table.

She was the only person sitting alone.

A small brass band were set up inside the café playing 'The Wedding Glide' over and over, and chirpy young men selling overpriced red roses seemed to be simply everywhere, circling the tables, all doing good business.

Well, good for them.

Posie started to read her mail, which consisted of a note from Suzannah saying 'A MAN IS TRYING TO CALL YOU, OVER AND OVER! VERY ANNOYING!' which was decidedly unhelpful, followed by an unrelated and single ripped-out piece of newspaper that had been stuffed inside a small blank envelope; also unhelpful.

Posie just had time to note that the page of newspaper was a week old, and from *The Norwich Mail*, and she had started to read its heading – 'NORFOLK MURDER…' – when suddenly the music and the circling waiters got too, too much for her to bear.

She stuffed everything back into her carpet bag and flounced out, like a proud girl who has been stood up by the lad of her dreams, and Posie walked city-bound, on and on, her nicest silver-sequinned Mary-Jane shoes pounding the sparklingly-cold frosted London pavements, until she found her feet taking her away from jostling, crowded Fleet Street.

Once or twice, she thought she was being followed; heard footsteps coming unaccountably close, almost mimicking her own. Once she thought she heard a man behind her, calling out her name. But each time, on turning, there had been no-one there; no-one specific.

Just crowds.

She dipped beneath the jutting dark-beamed Tudor overhang of the old pub which was always known as 'Prince Henry's Room', beneath which a parade of newsagents, cigarette shops and hairdressers were jammed together on the pavement, and then she pushed through the attendant crowds of gossiping customers in thick, lumpy mufflers. She rushed on under the elaborately carved stone entrance into the sudden and contrasting peace of Inner Temple Lane.

It was like stepping into another world.

Calm.

It was true that this space, the Inner Temple, a sort of vast private manicured garden surrounded by grand lawyers' offices, was always almost virtually silent.

You could practically hear the ice creak on the frozen trees.

Here the air held the peculiar centuries-old salty tang of the River Thames mixed with the perfumes of ancient, damp, curling parchment, and a few groups of crow-like black-gowned lawyers were standing about in sombre clusters on the grey cobbled corners, muttering together importantly, the cold seeming not to trouble them.

Posie had walked without really understanding her own motive or direction, but as soon as the body of the circular yellow-stoned Temple Church – a jewel of a place built eight hundred years ago by the all-powerful order of the Knights Templar – loomed up before her, she knew that her heart, rather than her head, had guided her here.

She almost wanted to cry out in relief, and the choke of that stab of recognition got stuck in her throat.

Walking around the buttresses of the church, which was impenetrable and solid as a castle, she headed for the side door, which was open, a flickering candle alight in the plain-glass lantern above it.

Coffee-time. It was a good time to take solace here.

Lunchtime Communion for the lawyers was not for another hour or so yet, and morning choir practice for the boy choristers of the church was obviously very much over, as evidenced by the pile of scarlet cassocks which were all stuffed in a pile on the bench just inside the door, hastily abandoned before the boys had rushed back to their school lessons.

A sheet of music fluttered on the floor, brittle as an autumn leaf.

In the half-darkness inside the church, a fuggy incense-laden warmth greeted her and Posie walked past a young, golden-haired German husband and wife who were holding identical Baedeker tourist guides, their arms wrapped tightly around each other as if worried the other might suddenly be cut adrift, as if in a storm.

Their furtive glancing eyes and almost-desperate longing for each other spoke of the bedroom rather than a routine historical outing, and, out of the blue, Posie felt a stab of jealousy.

Honeymooners, Posie thought to herself.

And then, rather disingenuously, she also thought: *That stage won't last long.*

The couple were pretending to intently study the stone effigies of some of the Templar Knights on the floor.

These monuments were impressive: prayerful warriors with tiny stone dogs carved at their spiked heels; unseeing eyes forever staring up at the rising dome of the church tower soaring way, way above. Medieval paintings in reds, blues and yellows circled the walls here with elaborate curves and foliage, and sad-eyed saints were placed even higher up, only just visible in the gloom.

Other than the golden-haired young couple, the church was completely empty.

Head bowed, Posie walked quickly to a point mid-way down the main nave, the ruby and sapphire and emerald stained-glass windows to her right catching the sunlight and throwing refractions across her face. Dodging the light shafts, she sat down quickly in a dark Victorian pew which seemed familiar; shadowy, close.

And now she was breathing the incense-heavy air and putting her huge old carpet bag - with all her work still inside - down on the stone floor by her feet.

She sat, eyes fixed straight ahead at the altar, where early spring flowers were placed around the golden cross: tiny, frozen, too-early daffodils, and twigs of witch-hazel mixed with boughs of lemon-yellow wintersweet, stripped back to the bare stalks. The zingy, lemony scent of the tiny flowers was strong, confusing: the perfume seemed to promise summer in a wintery world.

How different it all seemed here from how she remembered it.

Because in the recesses of her own mind, this was a place of darkness and music and spice-laden drinks and twinkling magic, a place permanently stuck in Christmas.

What had Posie's subconscious mind hoped for here in the Temple Church? Some kind of revelation? Guidance, perhaps on her current unhappiness?

Yes, maybe that was it; a lead towards a solution.

But that was ridiculous.

No solutions would be forthcoming. Because this place was not about now; its secrets were stories from Posie's past.

Part of a fairytale which had gone wrong.

Very wrong.

****

Two

As an adult, Posie always tried not to think about what had happened back then.

It had been easy. Busy as she was with her own work, and with her husband, and her babies Kit and Katie, and her darling little step-daughter, Phyllis, too, the days and weeks and months seemed to race along, and looking *back*, especially to difficult things, was a luxury she hadn't ever taken the time for.

Hadn't wanted to take the time for.

But now, perhaps, it was the right time.

Licking away her metallic red lipstick nervously, Posie tried to free her mind enough to let the memories come.

She began with the basics.

Every year the Parker family had travelled down from Norfolk for a special day out in London, the weekend before Christmas.

It was always the same: a visit to see the big Christmas tree in Trafalgar Square, and a dash around Hamleys Toy Emporium on Regent Street, and then afternoon tea with mince pies at a fancy hotel in Piccadilly.

Then on *here*. The candlelit carol concert.

For the first few years which Posie could remember, as a little girl, both parents had attended.

She recalled her mother, Rosa: beautiful, darkly exotic, eyes flashing, proud. Her long skirts a little too flouncy for her role in life as a provincial Vicar's wife, her hat just a little too frivolous, worn at a rakish angle. Puffs of dark hair.

Posie's father was clear in her mind, too. The Reverend Henry Parker: upright, older, golden-fair, handsome, decked out all in a big tweed cape, his dog-collar prominent against his black shirt. Shaking hands with everyone, beaming in the candle-lit darkness.

He'd been the Rector of an important benefice of five big churches up on the Norfolk coast, although his inherent laziness kept him stationed pretty much at his own, which was St Nicholas in Blakeney, a gorgeous gem of a church, with two peculiar towers and some fascinating medieval graffiti depicting ships lost at sea.

The Reverend Parker had it within his power to hand out posts within these five churches fairly often, which meant he was catnip to poverty-stricken young priests who were desperate for their first jobs.

Her father's loud voice had been reassuring, kindliness itself: *'Season's Greetings to you, my man… Who told you to speak to me, lad? Ah, yes: jolly fine fella. A position as curate? Look, here's my card: write to me, won't you? I'll reply in the New Year, it's very possible I have something coming up.'*

Posie closed her eyes now as if to conjure up that darkness again.

She remembered the excitement she and her own brother Richard had felt as they egged each other on, edging further towards the crib with its life-sized nativity figures: the silky skin of the figures painted in soft and lifelike gesso; the glass eyes sparkling like something real.

The spectacularly golden-haloed Mary in her blue satin, and the baby Jesus in his sumptuous green velvet swaddle were more beautiful than anything that the Parker children could ever imagine existing.

One year, being particularly daring, Posie had reached out and touched Mary's cheek and she could have sworn it was warm.

Posie wanted to laugh at her younger self now. Instead, she found she was crying, and she rubbed her tears away impatiently with her leather-gloved fingers, smudging powder and silver eyeshadow and Maybelline black mascara into a bleary mess.

Stupid tears.

For what?

For the loss of a belief in magic?

Whatever the case, the crib here had certainly been more beautiful than the roughly-hewn wooden figures which had been whittled out by local fishermen while out at sea, and which were brought out year after year in her father's coastal church in Blakeney; figures which were loved and cherished but which had certainly seen better days.

And if Posie concentrated hard enough she could almost smell again the treats served after the carol service here: the spiced orange punch with its cinnamon kick, the rich Christmas fruitcake which was cut into minute fingers for all the congregation.

She remembered that cake precisely, with its layer of proper marzipan, and a sliver of hard-frosted sugar icing, thick and rigid as days-old snow.

Posie could taste that icing now.

She remembered saving it, placing it in her handkerchief and then licking it on the train home, making it last the long, long journey back to Blakeney. Her brother Richard had usually eaten his up straightaway in the church itself, wolfing it down: he was that sort of a boy. Always hungry.

Every year he'd tried to steal Posie's own bit of cake, but he'd never succeeded.

The Parker family's connection with this place was tenuous; slender as a silver string of chance.

The reason they had come *here*, as opposed to any other number of carol concerts taking place across London the week before Christmas was purely a sentimental fancy.

Posie's father had been born the youngest son of a large country gentry family with five boys, and they had not been vastly wealthy at all. His lot, and his calling in life, had been the Church. He'd trained in Oxford, at Wycliffe Hall, and then spent a final year in London. One of his older brothers, a favourite, Edward, had trained as a lawyer.

The Inner Temple had been Edward Parker's workplace, and the Temple Church had been 'his' church. Edward Parker had even married here; a nice uncomplicated girl, Ruth, who had had the misfortune of dying in childbirth only a year after the wedding.

Edward and his young wife – pregnant and enthusiastic – had taken Henry Parker under their wing for the year that Henry was in London, inviting him to the Temple Church for services, including the carol service at Christmas.

The magic of the carol service had tapped into something in Henry Parker's rather traditional, sentimental character, and Posie's father had clung on doggedly to this London tradition, even after he left the capital. The tradition had become his very own.

He'd continued to attend every year here even after – and perhaps *especially* after – his successful brother Edward had died, tragically young, in the Boer War, ten years before Posie was born.

Edward's name was up here, gilded carefully on a too-high board, along with scores of others from the Inner Temple who had volunteered to fight; a so-called 'Roll of Honour.'

It was a happiness and a sadness for her father, Posie supposed, to have continued attending.

Henry Parker always made a point of knowing the Master of the Temple, who was effectively the Vicar in charge, trying to ensure a slight connection.

He'd continued to stay in touch with a few of his brother's legal colleagues too, who were always polite but distant in their manner, perhaps sensing a slight oddness about the Reverend Parker. Because nobody likes a needy hanger-on.

Posie realised now, from a distance of more than twenty years, that these carol concerts must have been utterly boring for her mother, Rosa, who would far rather have spent the preciously-short time in London in the shops.

Or, in fact, *anywhere* other than yet another dank, dark, cold church, of which Rosa saw enough in Norfolk.

And so these services had gone on every year for Posie as a little girl.

Eight years old; nine years old.

Ten…

But then came a big gap in Posie's memory.

A formative gap. Life-changing.

Things that were obscured. A gap of three years when the family had *not* attended here for the carol service.

These years fell like heavy coins into the pool of her memories now: 1903, 1904, 1905.

Posie struggled to fix the exact date when they had returned here. It must have been 1906, when she'd been fourteen. And her brother Richard would have been sixteen.

This time their tweedy-caped father was very present in the memory, his braying voice as loud as ever, but their mother, Rosa, was missing.

Rosa had been missing for the entirety of the gap of three years.

And she had gone on missing forever after.

The ongoing absence of a mother – *their* mother – had scarred the Parker children's lives at that point, for many reasons, and the local gossiping had been horrible, but the absence of Rosa Parker was most keenly felt far away from the Rectory, on 'public' outings, when they revisited traditions which had formerly contained her within them.

The first time they had returned here, after three years, it had been difficult to bear.

Posie and her brother, awkward ages anyhow, had hung back when their father had greeted people, those embarrassingly half-remembered legal colleagues, the simperingly hopeful new priests. The children had longed to be gone.

And then her brother Richard *had* gone.

Because another two years had flown past, and then he was at Cambridge, at university, and he was completely free. No longer at the beck and call of their father, he was able to stay up in college until virtually Christmas Eve, with only brief trips home.

Posie found she had covered her face with her hands now, as if for protection. She crouched down lower in the pew.

If the German couple walked past her, they would simply think she was praying. They wouldn't be able to see that she looked a mess; her face completely wet with tears, her eyes red and puffy, tears dripping off her nose.

She felt, like a weight, the sense of those lost years moving heavily onwards, sifting their patterns, until they found their eventual shape, kaleidoscope-like.

The kaleidoscope fixed at her destiny.

An unwanted and unasked for destiny; the stay-at-home, grown-up 'spinster' daughter. Young but pitiable.

During 1912 and 1913 Posie had still been living with her father at the Norfolk Rectory.

Blakeney was on a bleakly jagged and crumbling coast, a coast whipped by storms in which local fishing boats routinely went missing and whole crews perished. Where windmills punctuated the land like beacons and where silver seals basked on sandbanks. A place where the fiery pink sunsets were more beautiful than anywhere else on earth.

But Posie had been almost twenty years old in 1913 and her life was unfulfilled. She had been restless, cross, a mess of hot unguarded energy.

She'd seethed at the unfairness of her situation, not knowing how to resolve things.

The main problem was that she was uneducated; untrained for anything.

Before he went up to Cambridge, her brother Richard had been educated properly at Eton, whereas Posie had only ever had a Governess, and that had been patchy, and only when money had allowed.

Neither of her parents had ever thought it important for Posie to be sent to school, and she'd tried desperately to borrow off the back of her brother's extra holiday tuition.

Those at least were fond memories. As close to school as she'd ever got.

Posie smiled to recall herself sitting at the back of the hot pencil-scented schoolroom – really the old nursery – on the top floor of the Rectory for a snatch of six weeks every summer, where she'd lapped up Shakespeare and algebra and French verb conjugations much faster and more eagerly than her brother and his best friend, weedy little Lord Rufus Cardigeon, who stayed with them every summer, and whose father, the rather frightening Tenth Earl Cardigeon, actually paid for all the extra cramming in exchange for Rufus being boarded upon them.

The summer of 1907 was particularly vivid in the memory.

It seemed only yesterday that the two glassy-eyed boys were preparing, aged seventeen, for their university exams; they were frazzled, longing to be outside on the pine-fringed beach, or crabbing in the creek, or just playing cricket. Richard Parker had even deigned to teach Posie to ride a bicycle, and the three of them would skitter along the quayside, heading for open country, the boys on brand-new shiny black Royal Enfield Duplex's, and Posie riding whatever was available at the time. This was usually a very old and rusty Roadster which belonged to Ted, the Gardener's boy, who was terribly sweet on Posie.

Compared to these sun-drenched snatches of freedom, the boys were angry at having to sit inside at scratched children's desks, learning.

In Posie's mind's eye she saw their heads lolling, listless; bored eyes watching the trapped angry buzzing flies swarming on the big, sand-dusted windows. Sapped.

She recalled the young tutor, a decidedly handsome, floppy-haired, Byronesque teacher from Eton itself, trying to earn some extra money over the holidays, perhaps for his wedding?

He'd got crosser and crosser stationed over at the blackboard, with only fourteen-year-old Posie paying any sort of rapt attention to him at all.

She remembered the frustrated and pompous yelling of this tutor: 'Even this wretched *girl* has got the answers. A *girl*! Come on, lads. She's got her ruddy arm in the air the whole time and I'm doing my best to ignore it, but when she's the only blighter in here who knows what's happening that's dashed difficult. Perhaps *she* should go to Cambridge, eh? No? No, we can't have that happening. Dash it all, she's making you fellas look stupid. Sit up and bally well listen!'

Posie had mooned after this man for a bit, actually, and so his barb had stung, but still, he'd confirmed what in her mind she had always known. She was clever and she could certainly keep up.

And so she had taken what education she was able to. Pecked at it like a hungry bird.

Posie was angry about this even now, years and years later. Angry at her parents; angry at herself.

She felt the keen and precious anger of her younger self, all that roaring energy, and she tried to contain it now with the wisdom of womanhood.

She failed.

She'd never, *ever* let Katie, or Phyllis get into that position: she knew education was important, as was encouragement. With one you could get somewhere, but with both you could go everywhere.

By 1913 Posie had no shorthand, nor any skills at sewing or special needlework. Worse still, she was a young 'gentlewoman', being a Vicar's daughter, and therefore anything like shop work, or factory work, or office work was seen by her father as very much 'beneath' her, although frankly she would have seized on any opportunity and given it her all.

Blakeney itself was not much of an option for work though. It was a place in flux; and not in a good way.

When the Reverend Parker had accepted the post as Rector there, before Posie's brother was born, the town had still been a buzzing port awash with foreign dockers and merchants yelling out exciting, incomprehensible commands.

There had been huge boats moored tightly alongside the quayside, with horses and carts queuing up patiently to receive the unloaded cargos. The three public houses and full quota of shops and services had all been packed to the gunnels with sailors, doing a brisk trade.

But by 1913 the harbour had silted up, with bigger boats unable to get in, and the railway which reached to Holt, the nearest market town, had taken the place of the boats.

There were wild rumours in the town of a new hotel being built on the quayside, of trying to bring tourists to Blakeney with promises of golf and sailing and birdwatching, but nothing had happened yet.

The pubs and shops and blacksmiths were still open, but empty, drawing their last juddering breaths of certainty, and the men of the town were underemployed, listless, hanging around doorways, drinking too much, wretched.

Wanting more.

There was certainly nothing in Blakeney for Posie.

There had been a tiny bit of talk on her father's part about using his 'connections' and Posie working abroad as a Governess, or as a paid companion, but she had blanched at this.

It had sounded like a living hell of boredom.

And besides, by 1913 the Reverend Parker was becoming more eccentric, bordering on difficult. Sometimes he'd refuse to take his services in the week, sometimes even refusing to take the main Sunday service.

He seemed to hold things together when the Bishop of Norwich called on him every other month or so, but in truth, the Reverend Henry Parker was relying on his network of curates more and more. He'd spend long, long periods in his study, next to the fire, on the floor, playing with a Siamese cat he had inherited from a dead parishioner.

It was called Mr Minks and Posie's father let it climb the red velvet curtains in there.

He let it get away with murder.

Mr Minks hated men, mostly, which made his affection for Posie's father inexplicable. It tried to attack most male visitors to the house, whipping out a knife-sharp claw almost on the first meeting, often making things awkward and bloody. The Reverend Parker didn't seem to find this odd, or wrong, and sometimes laughed about the attacks, as if the cat might actually be a good and discerning judge of character.

Other things had been getting awkward, too.

Money in the house was getting tighter, and every spare penny which *wasn't* used on running the Rectory was sent to Richard, at Trinity College in Cambridge, where he was taking his doctorate, for studying and living.

For becoming a man.

Apparently.

And whilst the Parker family had fortunately been blessed with an excellent team of staff at the Rectory, Posie had wondered whether cuts in the household expenditure could be made in order to save money.

She suggested to her father that she, Posie, could become the Housekeeper, or, if this was unappealing, then Mrs Hickory, the Cook, could take over that role as well.

But the Reverend Parker had gone berserk at all this; accusing Posie of meddling, upsetting the equilibrium, especially when each servant was absolutely dependant on their wage in Blakeney's stutteringly awful economy.

After this rebuke Posie had left well alone.

Needing an occupation, Posie had tried to keep her eyes open to the world while she worked out what to do.

She'd taken *The Lady* as if her life depended on it, picking it up every week at the Post Office in the High Street, run by a Mr Joshua Parker, who was no relation, and really jolly nice, even if he was 'chapel' rather than part of her father's traditionally Anglican flock.

The pages of 'positions vacant' in *The Lady* had been a way of feeling close to an escape.

Several times Posie had filled out a blank telegram in reply to one of the advertisements: for shop work down in London, in Fortnum's, on the sweet-counter, or in Harrods, on the bloom-stall. But then she'd lost her nerve.

The telegrams had remained unsent. She burnt them later in the grate up in her bedroom, with anger and relief and resentment.

Posie grinned now as she sat in the Temple Church, her tears almost dry.

Thank goodness for Holt.

Because, growing bolder, the local market town had become a refuge.

Claiming a tiny stipend from her father of sufficient money for the bus fare to town and a hot drink while there, Posie had travelled once a week, on a Tuesday, into Holt on the Number 46 bus.

And that small journey, turning inland across rushy, canal-hatched beige flatlands where windmills and sailboats were the only visual treats, had proved some much-needed variety.

Ostensibly the trips to Holt were to use the Public Library, and with no real money in her purse, Posie would first wander the main street of this small, proud, flint-built market town for an hour or so.

She'd stare into the tantalizing windows of clothes shops; cake shops; Clabe, the jewellers; the two tiny hat shops.

She'd spend time looking in the huge windows of Neals, the popular and busy bicycle shop, where glossy baskets and bells and colourful paniers were out on display, together with perhaps the most spectacular bicycle Posie had ever seen: a second-hand ladies 'Golden Sunbeam', which was shiny black, with small, smart accents of gold, which looked like it was simply made for adventures.

But it cost twelve pounds, which was, for some in service, almost an annual salary. Certainly, it was more than most people in Holt could afford; a truly staggering amount.

Beyond what Posie could fathom.

But still she had looked at it every week, and the fact it had remained in the window, hers for the looking, was a pleasure in itself.

Likewise, the Department Store, Bakers & Larners, sold home-made boxes of chocolates which made Posie's mouth water, but they were also only hers for the looking.

Best of all were the windows of F. W. Baker, which was a glorified grocer, and sold everything. It always had a display of stationery, and its windows were full of blue Basildon Bond packages of expensive paper and envelopes, and, most magical of all, F. W. Baker also stocked silver-bound notebooks, complete with matching silver-papered pencils.

Silver!

It had always been her favourite colour.

One day, Posie had told herself, *I will use those every single day*.

She *did* use the Public Library, but not as her father imagined she might. She'd stock up hurriedly on a bagful of novels for the week, snatching them from the shelves willy-nilly.

Posie was much more interested in the newspaper section, housed in the hot, fusty Reading Room, where she could read about world events and what was going on away from Norfolk.

Here were all the big London newspapers which weren't available to her in Joshua Parker's Blakeney Post Office.

The Times, *The Telegraph,* the *Associated Press*. These and others were much pored over by Posie, devoured.

She'd read the bits about the Suffragettes first.

Brave deeds by brave girls: meetings and violence, placard-holding, marches, hunger strikes.

Posie read about what Emily Davies and the Pankhursts were up to all over the country: their attacks on the Prime Minister, and an attempt to bring down the King's horse at the Epsom Derby, which ended in sudden tragedy.

From the newspapers she learnt of local women's suffragette groups, and that there was, unbelievably, a group in Norwich, Norfolk's biggest city.

This group had a headquarters on London Street, and there were often photographs of the members standing outside their office: bright-faced vivid girls with sleek dark hair, bearing flags and banners and parasols, grinning for the cameras.

The Norwich suffragette group held a big demonstration in the city centre in the summer of 1913, and although there were lots of photographs, it didn't come to much. The neighbouring group at Great Yarmouth were braver, bolder: they set fire to the pier in their town to get a bit of attention, and in that, they succeeded.

Posie supported all of this in her heart, even the burning of the pier, and she would dearly have loved to join in.

But without a job and living entirely according to her father's rules meant she didn't have the financial means to travel to the impossibly far-off Norwich, let alone to stay for a march or law-breaking of some sort. Even if she had been allowed a bicycle, it would have been too far to ride.

It was all totally out of the question. Complicated.

She bit her lip now, in the Temple Church.

'Stupid little beggar. I *should* have been there. Should have been a Suffragette. I should have found a way.'

But her mind was running backwards again, to 1913, to the Reading Room in the library at Holt...

Posie recalled how she had liked the true crime pages best of all in the newspapers: national roundups which included fascinating reports of cold cases and diligent police work.

Sometimes there were the court transcripts from big murder trials, including the Judge at the end, summing up, and these covered the motive at the heart of each case.

It seemed that motive usually boiled down to one of two things: money, or love.

Rarely, but sometimes, it was both.

Posie saw her earnest twenty-year-old self, making careful notes in her small cheap pocketbook, hoping to follow the crime stories through in the next week or so, as they reached, or didn't reach, their resolutions.

It had felt thrilling.

She'd kept a keen eye out for jobs, too.

Once, and it had almost popped out of the pages of the *Associated Press* at her, Posie had seen an advertisement which was utterly perfect.

It was an advert placed by New Scotland Yard – in the very heart of London – for a lady policewoman's course.

She'd almost fallen off her Reading Room chair in excitement.

It had read:

<u>TEN LADIES REQUIRED FOR TRAINING AS SPECIAL POLICE ASSISTANTS (PAID POSITIONS)</u>

ALL APPLICANTS WELCOME, REGARDLESS OF BACKGROUND (ALTHOUGH LADIES WILL REQUIRE GOOD PASSES IN ASSESSMENTS FOR HEALTH, EYESIGHT AND READING/WRITING).

FIVE FOOT ONE MINIMUM HEIGHT REQUIREMENT, AND NO CRIMINAL RECORD.

BICYCLE EXPERIENCE NOT ABSOLUTELY NECESSARY, BUT THE SKILL IS PREFERRED.

APPLICANTS MUST BE HEARTY, ROBUST AND UNAFRAID. ESPECIALLY OF BLOOD AND DEATH AND THE UNKNOWN.

(TWO PROFESSIONAL REFERENCES ESSENTIAL.)

This description had left Posie quite breathless.

HEARTY, ROBUST AND UNAFRAID?

She was all of that, and much, much more.

She fitted this advertisement to a T. She could even ride a bicycle.

This is my opportunity, she'd told herself, copying the advert out carefully into her pocketbook with a pounding heart, then reading and re-reading it in the bus stop outside Gresham's School at the edge of Holt Market Square, before she'd caught the bus home again.

She cherished it to herself, like a nugget of secret hope.

Here was an opportunity to get involved in myriad investigations of criminal work on a daily basis, and to get paid for it!

On the bus ride home she had imagined herself flying around London on a gleaming black bicycle, – perhaps a Golden Sunbeam? – with her perfectly-imagined new leather satchel streaming out behind her, filled with silver notebooks, dashing from one case to another, with a pack of another nine fearless girls all fanning out alongside her.

Unafraid.

Free, enjoying an independence all of her own making.

Then reality had set in.

She *wasn't* free to simply 'leave' her father's house; he'd never agree to her working for the police, and never, over his dead body, would he allow her to live alone in London.

And besides, who on earth would provide her with a professional reference?

She'd have trouble finding one.

Let alone two.

She had no-one to ask, and she couldn't simply make it up.

She couldn't ask one of the curates; they would rat on her to her father. Although a nice one *had* just started, who looked like he was kind. Funny-looking, but kind.

But he barely knew Posie, and why on earth would he risk his career to help her?

Posie only really had one good friend, Hattie Draper. They'd meet for tea twice a month in the plush lounge of the Feathers Hotel in Holt.

Hattie was a dispenser in Drozier's pharmacy on the Cromer Road; a clever, tiny slip of a girl, living off her wits. She was an orphan, but with a good education behind her, which had been funded by a sensible spinsterish great-aunt.

Posie had met Hattie while buying eye-drops in the pharmacy, on one of her first regular trips into the town, and they had struck up an instant friendship.

Hattie was one of those girls who were always exquisitely groomed, with a penchant for red; it contrasted so well with her unusually jet-black hair.

She normally tried to match her cheap enamel earrings to whatever daring shade of lipstick she felt like wearing that day, and the subtlest was the colour of a blazing poppy field in May.

Hattie had been responsible for persuading Mr Drozier to stock Maybelline's line of four coloured lipsticks, one of which was the poppy red, and, so far, it had been a stroke of genius on her part.

The small range of lipsticks had become a raging success: Mr Drozier couldn't get stock in fast enough, and new customers came in daily specifically for the make-up, which now had its own proud little display in the window.

Sales of lipsticks had overtaken that of stockings, and Hattie had been given a small raise.

Hattie presented Posie with a lipstick as a birthday present once, and, although it was a soft and unobtrusive pink, it had remained in its metal case unused, untouched, ever after. Posie hadn't had Hattie's reserves of courage.

Posie had been sure Hattie would know what to do regarding the references.

But Hattie had shaken her head mournfully, licked at her red lipstick nervously.

'Golly, this *does* look right up your street. But dash it all, I can't help, Posie. Did you think *I* could give you a reference? I'm the lowest of the low, certainly not *professional*. If this was for me, I could get old man Drozier to write a reference, although he probably wouldn't, as he'd know he'd be losing me. Or else I'd ask one of the older ladies in Norwich, at the women's group I've just joined, to write a reference. A couple of them are 'professional' in the true sense: lawyers, doctors, midwives.'

'A women's group? You mean…?'

‘That’s right.’ Hattie had pointed quickly and proudly at a tiny pin worn high on her bosom: ‘VOTES FOR WOMEN.’

‘Oh! Oh, of course.’

It turned out that in the relatively short time Posie had known her, Hattie had become a fully signed-up member of the suffragette’s group in Norwich, although she’d only managed to get along a few times, and Hattie admitted that any ‘vim’ in the group seemed to have long gone, with the meetings being rather disappointingly shallow.

‘I should have joined it years back, shouldn’t I?’ sighed Hattie. ‘That’s when they had fire in their bellies. Too late for all that now. But look here: don’t brood like the dickens about this advert, Posie. Don’t huff. There must be a way around it, eh? What about that fancy rich fella you told me about? Your brother’s pal? That Lord so-and-so? You can’t get better than a real-life Lord on your application, can you?’

‘Rufus, you mean?’

And in a flurry of manic desperation, Posie had then written to her brother’s best friend, Lord Rufus Cardigeon, her old pal from the summer classroom.

He was still at Cambridge then himself, and she’d asked him if he might do the honours, but he hadn’t even had the decency to write back, and Posie had felt dreadful afterwards, slighted. Foolish.

She wondered now at this.

Why had Rufus, with whom she was still very much in touch, never spoken to her about it? It had taken some nerve on Posie’s part to write that letter and its lack of reply still stung, across the years.

Posie vowed that in her next telephone call to Rufus she would dredge it up and have it ‘out’ with him.

Why should she be the only one for whom the past came calling?

Posie sat up now in the Temple Church, focussing.

The German honeymooners were kissing in a dark corner of a pew on the opposite side to her, slurpily, hands all over each other, their Baedeker guidebooks abandoned on the floor. They either didn't care, or else they thought they were unobserved.

Posie tried not to turn and stare.

A portly, square-headed young man in a suit with a surplice thrown over the top suddenly appeared up near the altar. He was hurriedly hunting through thick folios of music with a deep frown on his dog-like face.

He had the frantic air of one who has lost something important. He had obviously come in through a hidden door near the altar, quiet as a cat. He didn't give Posie or the German lovers a second glance, smoothing his moustache down frequently, lost in his scores. The organist? The choirmaster? A curate?

Posie had known plenty of curates. They had come and gone with great regularity at her father's Rectory and Sunday dinners had never been complete without at least two of them in attendance. Most of them had been dull.

But Posie's thoughts were pulling her backwards again, back to that hopeful advert in the *Associated Press* which had made her twenty-year-old heart judder so.

New Scotland Yard.

It was almost funny, really. What a coincidence that she was now married to the most senior policeman there…

Funny too that she had never spoken of the advert to him, and she vowed she would go and look it up again when she had time, in the archives of the *Associated Press*. Posie knew the editor, Sam Stubbs. He would find it for her. It would be very easy.

She would like to read it again, with fresh and experienced eyes. She'd show it to Lovelace, and they'd laugh about it.

Or maybe not.

She wondered suddenly who the ten successful women

had been? Were they still at the Yard? And in what capacity? Would Richard Lovelace, her husband, know who they were? Would he even care?

They must be her own age now.

He had certainly never mentioned them, and Posie had never met any lady policewomen there. Unless they were kept carefully away from her by Richard?

Unless…

Unless one of them wore an amber musk of a fragrance.

She shut the thought down quickly.

That advert had given her so much hope back in 1913. But it had caused her so much pain, too.

It had been a bitter pill to swallow, but having exhausted all avenues of possibility in finding a reference, slowly, slowly she had let the dream go.

Tried to accept the absolute and daily reality of her life.

She'd felt a peculiar kind of low at the carol service of 1913.

Here, at this very church.

Posie had come alone with her father, her brother being too busy. They hadn't known then that their lives would shortly be changing again, and forever.

The service in 1913 had been less ostentatious than usual. There had been no crib.

In the place where the dog-faced man was now searching for his music there had been only a few candles placed around for decoration, and sprigs of holly with no berries. Fewer candles than ever before.

Instead, there had been sombre talk of war: talk of political unrest, of allegiances made and honoured, of storm clouds ahead.

There had been no mulled wine, no fingers of fruitcake. No-one to fight for the icing with, either.

Times were changing: it was in the driven icy wind.

As her father had spoken with the Master of the Temple and a bevy of eager young clergymen after that bleak little service, she'd sat on alone in a dark pew.

Perhaps it had actually been *here*?

In which case this was the exact spot where Posie had vowed to change things.

To turn her life around.

To become stronger, and bolder; not just through her choice of lipstick. To be more like Hattie, but more ruthless.

There was to be no more reliance on her father, whom she had started to suspect of actually being quite mad.

She needed to get *away*.

It had been time to act.

* * * *

Three

In the library Reading Room at Holt, in among the tall reedy spinsters and bowler-hatted old gentlemen in mothball-scented coats, twenty-year-old Posie Parker had noticed a man.

He was young, clean-looking, unremarkable.

His clothes were winter-fresh and cut from a very fine Harris Tweed. He wore a waistcoat and a proper gold fob watch. He looked expensive and he smelt of lemon soap.

He carried a black briefcase filled with documents and his slicked-down mid-brown hair was combed carefully.

His hands had long fingers like a piano player and trim clean nails, but they were calloused underneath from a sport like cricket, or rowing: Posie knew the signs. He wore a signet ring on his left-hand little finger with the carved initials 'HB'.

Apart from the ring, and his eyes, which were almost a purplish-grey behind owlish horn-rimmed spectacles, he was plain as plain could be.

He always came in to the library Reading Room at the same time as Posie was there. Five minutes before midday.

And Posie had the distinct impression that he came there because of *her*.

Over a few weeks, when the days were getting much

darker, starting up around the time of All Hallows Eve, she became suddenly conscious of this young man's eyes on the back of her neck as she read.

She turned sometimes, trying to catch his eye, fiddling with the long tendrils of her thick dark hair which escaped from her bun. All 'accidentally on purpose'.

He would tend to stay ten, fifteen minutes, then leave, throwing a last hungry look her way. He never spoke to her, never touched his hat to her. Not once. By Advent of 1913 not one word had passed between them.

And so after Christmas Posie took it upon herself to force it along.

The young man would always take up a position near the exit door, and one dark January day when he had just arrived, Posie hurriedly crammed on her hat and coat and gloves, picked up her ancient satchel and dropped a short, ready-prepared note right in front of him, atop his *Daily Mail*.

She then rushed out.

The note read:

Sir,

Luncheon? In fifteen minutes? Bakers & Larners main restaurant?

My name is Posie. I don't know your name.

(Please throw this note away. If you don't come, please do not try and speak to me about this ever again.)

It was a bold, bold move on her part. Part of the campaign for boldness.

First, would he even accept her invitation?

And secondly it was bold because Posie had barely enough money on her for a cup of tea in the very smart Department Store, let alone enough for lunch for two.

Also, Holt was her father's local town, even if he did hardly ever come here. Heaven forbid that one of her father's parishioners saw her unaccompanied with a strange young man; it would have become instant and undesirable gossip, spread all around the five churches. Her reputation would have been ruined.

As it turned out, things went smoothly.

The young man accepted her invite. As she had thought he would.

He arrived right on time, and flashed her a shy, wonder-filled smile, and paid for everything.

He was the perfect gentleman from the off.

'I'm Harry. Harry Briskow. Look here, I'm so pleased you dropped me that note. You know, I've actually been meaning to... Well, I saw you once, weeks ago; stepping off a bus. I thought I'd never seen such a jolly beautiful girl in all my life. And I'm afraid to say I followed you. I saw you looking in the bicycle shop, and then at the stationary. I found out where you go every Tuesday. I followed you, and waited. Have done so each week. I hoped I might pluck up the nerve to... well, the nerve to ask you for luncheon. Like *this*.'

Posie found his interest in her decidedly charming.

He was different to anyone else in her immediate circle. Unlike *her* family, his family were rich, and without any drama.

Harry was twenty-eight, the fifth of six sons. He liked sports, but his passion was cricket. He cycled every weekend and liked to drive his brand-new motor car. He was one of the first young men to have a motor vehicle, and his excitement was still palpable.

His father was the locally-important Sir Peregrine Briskow, a man whose family had got rich on boots and boot polish and bootlaces, many generations back.

Sir Peregrine was something of a local bigwig in Holt; the trustee of many committees and a presence on several charity boards.

Posie had seen Sir Peregrine's name in the newspapers as she had grown up; heard her father throw out a reference from time to time to 'Old Boots Briskow' in a half-contemptuous, half-grudgingly respectful sort of manner.

Harry's older brothers included a banker, a local doctor, a professional soldier, and the very eldest brother had done what was expected of him, taking over the family factory near Sheringham.

Harry laughed when explaining it: 'My father wanted a son in every profession. He wanted to get the Briskow name everywhere, and he almost holds a full hand!'

Harry had gone into the law at his father's say-so.

Fortunately, he loved it. The regulations and testy arguments which were his daily bread and butter as a solicitor were exactly the tools Harry loved to play with best. He was, as it turned out, a stickler for the rules.

A straight bat, but wielded strongly. That was his mantra. He said it at least once on every occasion Posie met him.

He worked for the local firm of solicitors on the Market Square, Marchpane & Marchpane, although there was only one Marchpane left, Regulus, and he was at least as old as Sir Peregrine himself and holding the fort alone.

Regulus Marchpane had recently and rather reluctantly accepted Harry's proposal of buying a half-share in the business.

Soon the firm would become Marchpane & Briskow.

The Marchpanes, Posie was given to understand, had always been in some sort of competition with the Briskows; the Marchpanes being a much older, but poorer, family, and the Briskows had all but stamped them out.

There was not very much left of the Marchpane inheritance.

Indeed, Sir Peregrine Briskow and his family of sons lived in a house which had originally been a Marchpane property until fifty years ago, when Regulus' father had been forced to sell.

Holly House was a vast red-brick civil war house just off the Market Square, built in a style much like a very grand dolls house, of the sort that little girls can only dream of.

Perhaps it was this odd and slightly chequered history, but it seemed to Posie that sadness oozed from Holly House, and the glittering mullioned windows reminded her of a hundred crying eyes.

The house was big enough, apparently, to contain – in great comfort – all the Briskows, and their wives, and the full quota of servants and underlings that such a big multi-generational house entailed.

Once she knew the prize at hand, which was essentially a good degree of wealth, and comfort, and prestige, Posie played to win.

She got bolder.

Thinking back now, aged almost thirty-four, Posie felt her face burn at the sheer audacity and single-mindedness of her ambition back then. She now felt a deep wholehearted remorse at that behaviour.

Perhaps it was one of the reasons this memory was buried so deep?

Because this whole operation had been nothing to do with love.

It had been calculated.

Harry, kind at heart, wealthy and reliable, overshadowed by the merits and looks of his more dashing brothers, had been hers for the taking.

With the benefit of hindsight, Posie wondered if her youthful self, so desperate to be away from her father's Rectory, had ever really understood the repercussions of the game she was playing in Holt?

Because although Harry *had* represented a way out, Posie's eventual position as his wife would have been a simple swap in circumstance, not a freedom. Kind though he was, she would have come full-circle: a woman living in a house which wasn't hers, with nothing to do and with no means of earning money.

She wouldn't have been in control of anything; still less her own destiny.

But the older Posie recognised that this sort of understanding had been far, far removed from the younger Posie's thoughts back then.

And so a flurry of courtship took place, with walks upon the pier at Cromer, and shopping sprees in Holt which left Posie giddy with disbelief at the presents an adoring Harry heaped upon her: a silver fox fur; a carpet bag in a dark red and black weave from Bakers & Larners; a big pile of the silver notebooks she coveted from F. W. Baker, together with a stash of the matching silver-papered pencils.

One day a special and rather cumbersome delivery had arrived at the Rectory, on the back of a cart, wrapped in black tarpaulins and string, and looking very mysterious.

The carter's boy asked for Posie; said it was a gift for her.

The lad struggled to lift the item down, and when he did, removing the wrappers, the 'Golden Sunbeam' bicycle was revealed in all its shining glory; a beacon of gorgeousness glowing out on a dark midwinter's day.

Posie gasped in befuddled delight, snatching the note tied to the handlebars.

PERHAPS WE CAN RIDE TOGETHER SOMETIMES? NOW I'M ONLY HALF AN HOUR FROM YOU WITH YOUR NEW WHEELS.

***YOUR VERY BEST,
HARRY.***

Soon she met Harry's family.

She was invited for afternoon tea at Holly House on a

cold Sunday afternoon in mid-March, and Posie arrived in her best brown tweed suit, carrying herself ramrod-straight and with a smile fixed in place. Desperate to impress.

Something seemed to be going on in the very bowels of the house though, and she thought she heard raised voices as she stood outside on the doorstep. A shout?

But she was led by a smiling parlourmaid down ringing white-and-black tiled passageways into an empty green-painted parlour with long, long windows which ran from floor to ceiling.

Posie realised that these were the exact same windows which made the house look as if it had eyes, but she tried to tamp that rather odd thought down and to concentrate.

She looked about her while she waited.

The parlour had a very old stuccoed ceiling with angels and devils fighting over a landscape which was unmistakeably Holt, with the Norfolk Broads and windmills and flatlands rendered exquisitely.

A particularly angelic cherub with a halo of holly held a golden key aloft, and he looked to be valiantly seeing off a whole pack of ferocious red-eyed wolves, who were baying at his tiny feet.

Dark hunting pictures adorned the walls, such as you might find in a gentleman's club, and there were ancient oak fitted window seats under each of those unnerving long windows, replete with green velvet cushions atop each one.

It was a truly horrible room.

Posie turned, to be confronted by what seemed a sudden gaggle of people, led by a buoyant Harry.

He was buzzing, excited, proud.

'Darling, Posie: now you simply *must* meet everyone…'

The occupants of the house stood awkwardly, ranged about her, crammed in like so many porcelain dolls, with an atmosphere that was more appropriate for a wake.

An unexpected but collective hostility buzzed at Posie

like a force-field, and she almost gasped at the strength of it.

What on earth had she done wrong?

Or had she walked into some terrible family crisis of which she, as yet, knew nothing?

But she'd bluster on.

As she always did.

And while Harry made the introductions, a young, ginger, blotchy-faced parlour-maid who went by the name of Millie bobbed about the place with platters of tiny fresh cakes and a teapot, looking out-of-sorts.

In fact, she looked as if she had been crying.

Millie fretted about the place, passing cups and saucers silently and almost fearfully to a tall, thin, reedy woman with a head of frizzy bright red hair lashed under a plain black cap, and Posie assumed that this was the taciturn but efficient Housekeeper, whom Harry sometimes spoke about, a Mrs Noakes.

A very tall man in his fifties, with a decidedly military bearing was decked out as the Butler, but Posie had the feeling he ran the whole place with an iron rod, and occasionally he would glance over at Millie, ensuring her service was up to scratch.

Once he patted the girl very quickly on the arm.

He was addressed as 'Wykham'.

Sir Peregrine 'Boots' Briskow was a small and narrow-faced man in his late fifties with sharp, flashing black eyes, and a quick, almost mincing step. In another life he could have been a dancer. He had big 'mutton chop' side whiskers and a very bald head, and an overarchingly pompous manner.

He obviously didn't relish the prospect of a Vicar's child as a future wife for his clever lawyer son, and it seemed to Posie that he did his very best to put her off from the start.

He smoked a battered pipe and told Posie morbid tales about Holly House itself; of its Catholic past with its hidden chambers for priests to escape through in the dangerous days of the civil war.

'There was some old legend about how one of these Catholic priest fellas got stuck in a hole here in the last year of the civil war and was never found. He had his dog with him, apparently. Not that *that* did him any good. Poor sop, eh?'

Sir Peregrine laughed as if he was telling a good joke.

He carried on: 'The Marchpanes were terrible at passing on the secrets of these old tunnels. We have no idea where any of them are. Some folk think the tunnels lead out from under the house and come up under the marshlands far away from the town itself, in the pinewoods near the sea. When the boys were little lads they tried to find out; drawing up maps and setting off around the house with screwdrivers and suchlike, but my Emily was always against it. She thought legends and curses should be left well alone. She was superstitious. "Let sleeping dogs lie," she'd say. Which was funny, as one of the ghosts in this house is supposed to be a black dog, and you only see it if your time is up: an omen of the hastening end…'

He paused theatrically, then exclaimed gleefully: 'WOOF! WOOF!'

The old man stared at Posie in a mocking way, as the whole room hushed into an absolute silence.

But Posie was used to dealing with her own father, who was as eccentric as they came, and she didn't bat an eyelid.

'How jolly, sir. I suppose you would like *me* to reveal that I have seen just such a dog here today, sir? But, alas, I have seen no dog. Neither living nor dead. You cannot spook me with your stories of ghosts, sir. I am unafraid.'

Sir Peregrine gave a thick chuckle.

'You have spirit, Miss Parker, which is good. My wife did, too. She looked like you, actually, my Emily. But with a much better figure; at least at first, before all the babies. And she had better eyes. Iris-coloured.'

Posie was taken aback at Sir Peregrine's rudeness, and so she was surprised when he suddenly came closer to her, spoke in a whisper: 'I have to go, I need to prepare for a Board Meeting in the morning. It was nice to meet you. You seem to be a girl with a peculiarly vivid personality. It is good, of course, to be unafraid. We must all try and stay that way, eh?'

Sir Peregrine muttered under his breath before leaving and it sounded like: 'Oh, *Emily...*'

Posie felt she had almost won him over.

She turned to Harry's brothers.

The eldest, Peregrine Junior, was known as Perry by all, and he was charm itself.

He had also struck lucky by way of looks: big and strong, with a splendid square face and golden hair, he had a wide white smile, and the warrior-like demeanour normally only found in the realm of renaissance artworks. He had the same purple-grey eyes as Harry; but his were large and full of his own self-worth, not hidden behind thick lenses. If Michaelangelo's David had suddenly sprung alive, Perry could have given him a run for his money.

Perry was obviously wasted running the family boot business. He should have gone further afield, where his beauty and confidence would get him far.

The second son, a doctor, Joseph, was different again: quiet and lithe and fatigued; he was serious, with sad black eyes. In his manner he was polite and he smiled as he chatted, but there was obviously something he was holding back, that was for sure.

The fourth son was the banker, Johnny, and he looked like a less-beautiful Perry, but he was coarser, and too loud; a joker with a sly, mocking manner, like his father.

Two brothers, both still unmarried, were absent. The third brother, Geoffrey, the professional soldier, was out in India, and Miles, the sixth and youngest brother, was a teacher at the local prep school, Greshams, where he was on duties in the boarding house every Sunday.

However, it was the wives of the three attendant brothers whom Posie found the most unnerving.

They sat crammed in a row on one of the window seats and they hardly responded to her polite chit-chat at all.

First was big, buxom, handsome Gwendoline, Perry's wife, with her mass of freckles and dark coppery hair and a small carved cameo at her frothy-laced throat.

'How delightful to meet you,' she said sharply, with a clipped delivery which dripped with sarcasm.

Gwendoline kept consulting her wrist-watch. She was keen to point out that she sat on the board of the local orphanage, and there was work to be done. She obviously didn't like wasting a single second, not even on a Sunday.

Next up was Girvan, Joseph's wife, who was dark and tiny, and very conscious of her own beauty and power.

She was like an evil sprite in one of Arthur Rackham's twisted fairytale pictures, although in reality, as she rather begrudgingly told Posie, she was a midwife, and she'd kept working despite her marriage.

Posie noticed her highly unusual black spinel engagement ring.

It flickered and flashed in the half-green light in an eerie, mesmerising way, but by far the most interesting thing about Girvan was her tiny silver pin, no bigger than a fingernail, enamelled in cream, green and violet, the same as Hattie's, with its tiny outrage 'VOTES FOR WOMEN' worn unconcealed beneath the broderie anglaise of her blouse.

The friendliest woman, in as much as she offered a smile, was plain-faced Kate, Johnny's wife, who was very heavily pregnant with the couple's first child, a first grandchild for Sir Peregrine.

Kate, who had been a teacher before her marriage, was full of frothy talk of the imminent baby and it was an easy – if not enlightening – conversation with which to join in.

Posie immediately and privately nicknamed these

women 'the Coven', and hoped against hope that she could smash through their icy exteriors and find a warmth hidden away there, somewhere. Because if she was to continue with Harry, and muddle along in this house, it would be easier to seek out friendships, rather than holding onto grudges.

And as Posie said goodbye, relieved to leave at last, she could have sworn that Girvan, in her quick Northern Irish accent, had muttered "… and shame the devil," at which Gwendoline had elbowed her sister-in-law quickly in the ribs.

Did they mean *her*, Posie Parker? Why the blazes was *she* a devil?

And even though Posie couldn't actually really and truly contemplate living at Holly House, and joining this strange group of women, things moved on quickly.

Harry was a fast worker.

He went to meet the Reverend Parker unannounced, and Posie's father was in for a surprise one blustery April afternoon when Harry turned up in his immaculate blue Ford 'Model T' motor-car, ostensibly to ask for Posie's hand in marriage.

Her father almost dropped his beloved cat.

'*What*, sir? You're asking what? You're who? A Briskow? My daughter, you say? Posie? *Marriage*?'

The Reverend Henry Parker was shocked, angry, insulting.

He claimed he knew nothing of Posie's 'gadding about', still less her morally-questionable adventures with local young men. He asked Harry to leave.

'Hear me out, sir.'

Harry Briskow pressed his suit confidently, there and then, and he was so eminently suitable that there was very little to complain about, and the Reverend Parker's initial reluctance was worn down remarkably quickly.

A week later the Reverend Parker gave his half-reluctant consent, and a small celebratory party was arranged to be held at the Rectory in May, and Posie's brother Richard had come back from Cambridge specially, right before his final doctoral exams.

All of the Briskow family were invited around to drink pale sherry in the parlour of the Blakeney Rectory and to eat a large iced ginger cake made with enthusiasm - if not skill - by Mrs Hickory, the Cook.

Posie was dreading the party but on the day itself everything seemed to go to plan.

Sir Peregrine was on top, falsely-jolly form, mainly confining himself to talking to Posie's father about the business matters in the area: fishing and farming quotas and the like; things which the Reverend Parker was not as well-informed about as he should have been.

Posie's brother, Richard, took over this conversation, steering it calmly, playing host beautifully, and covering any gaps and cracks.

He was impressive and Posie felt relieved. She overheard her brother telling Sir Peregrine that their mother had died years before.

Yes. It was a shame.

The Briskow brothers and Posie's brother argued and laughed about sport, about the likelihood of an English win at Wimbledon, and Perry in particular seemed to take up all the space in the room with his power and good cheer.

It all went fairly smoothly, and even the Coven formed a row and admired the views from the parlour's huge bay windows, with their vista of the bay, the sliver of glittering grey sea beyond, the boats tethered under an immense sky.

At least in May the Rectory wasn't absolutely freezing, and Posie had even managed to hide Mr Minks away in her father's study beforehand, rather than risk any surprise attacks.

Hattie Draper arrived halfway through, her black hair all mussed up, having got a puncture in her bicycle tyre on the way over, and she chattered about this with Harry for a bit before recognising Girvan from 'the group' and cloistering herself in a corner with her; their talk all about 'action', and 'protest.'

Hattie seemed to be having a lovely old time.

A sapphire and diamond engagement ring ('the colour of your beautiful eyes, my darling') was 'presented' by Harry to Posie at this party and shown around proudly. Even the three young Briskow wives were wide-eyed at the beauty of it.

'Green-eyed monster got their tongues, Miss Posie,' nodded Mrs Hickory later, self-importantly. 'I saw 'em when I was clearing up them cake-plates. They never saw a gem like it 'afore, I'll warrant. Especially that dark girl what looks like she's suckin' on a lemon. She's just got a horrible black pebble on her finger; evil-lookin' it is. 'Ere, show us again, Miss. What a sparkler, eh? I ain't seen nuffink like it 'afore.'

Posie didn't quite dare to meet her fiancé's purple-grey eyes at the party. In fact, she found the heaviness of his attention slightly wearing.

Harry watched for her at every second as she moved about, chattering away to his relations. He behaved like an anxious parent watching a child try to swim: as if she might fall back into deep water at any point; as if he might not be able to save her.

She flashed a grin at him.

I can manage this.

He grinned back, shrugged ruefully, smoked in relief, joined the Coven at the window, chattered about the beauty of Blakeney with Hattie.

After the Briskow family departed and she'd helped the maid and Mrs Hickory to clear the party things away, Posie walked with her brother by the creek, arm in arm, and they both watched the fishermen mending their nets.

The sky was mottled pink and a strange apricot light looked as if it was burning behind the clouds.

Richard Parker was about to leave again for Cambridge and Ted, the Gardener's lad, was already waiting with the horse and trap prepared, to take him on to Sheringham for a train over to King's Lynn, from where he would connect to Cambridge.

'By Gad, how beautiful it is here, Posie. You can't believe there's anything wrong in the world, can you? When you see a sky like that?'

He paused, bit at his lip.

'But awful things happen everywhere. Look here, I overheard a fella on the train today telling the Guard that his pal was a local policeman. This policeman swore on his life that a girl was found in the pinewoods near Sheringham last week, bludgeoned to death. Worse, actually. She was unrecognisable. A woman of ill repute, it turned out, but it makes no difference, does it? Poor lass. This policeman pal said other prostitutes have been going missing over the last few months, but their disappearances haven't been reported, due to their lowly status. It's all been kept out of the papers, of course. Hush-hush.'

'Gracious. That's terrible.'

'I'll say. So, for goodness' sake don't walk out at night, Posie. Not even with that nice Hattie… and don't ride out, either.'

He kicked out at an old lobster pot left on the pavement.

'Bad times are coming, Po. Generally, I mean.'

'Oh?'

'Mnnn. We both know Pa is getting odder. He's not right, is he? I've often felt guilty; leaving you with him here. That obviously isn't any way for you to live. We both know you've got to make your own way in the world, since there's no money for you. But, well…'

Richard stopped. 'Time is precious, Posie. Don't fill it up with nonsense.'

Her brother suddenly held Posie by the arms, as if he might never see her again, and he came out with it all in a rush.

'I say, Posie. No date has been set yet, has it? No wedding date, I mean? Look here, I rarely agree with our father on anything, as you know, especially these days, but well, this time it's different. Father telephoned me last week specially, you know? And then I spoke to him about it earlier and he was quite lucid. He kept telling me Harry was wrong. I agree. He's a lovely fella, but he's drippy. He'll never understand you: it will be our parents' story all over again. You're like Mama was. In fact, I've come to the conclusion recently that the only man in the world who could match you in spirit would be old Rufus Cardigeon, but of course, that's dashed impossible. Because he's… he's…'

Posie's whole being flared through with a stinging and palpable anger.

'What are you talking about? *Rufus?* Why on earth couldn't I be together with Rufus? Because he's too good for me, you mean? Or because he's a Lord? And I'm a nothing? Well, that's exactly the trouble. *I am a nothing.*'

And then, hot tears stinging her cheeks, Posie slapped her brother around the face with all the force she could muster, Harry's chunky glittering sapphire ring digging into the flesh deeply.

'*Ow!* POSIE! Holy…'

The subject was not raised again, but Posie was disagreeably conscious of the words which had passed. Her brother's words *and* her father's words.

It set going in her mind a tiny niggling doubt; a minute pin-sized hole in a carefully-tended net of calm.

Weeks later it was almost midsummer, and Posie walked with Harry along the coast from Cley back to Blakeney one baking-hot Saturday afternoon.

They walked hand in hand over the dried-up mudbanks where the sea and sky blurred in heat shimmers all around them.

The air was scented with amber hay and clean washing, but stronger than all of that was the intense salt of the sea.

Suddenly a windy squall blew up from nowhere.

Grass and sand whipped about them, and the masts of boats clanged.

A storm was coming. Quickly.

Harry was annoyed, and stared to the horizon. 'Looks like rain.'

He blew out his cheeks. 'I hope it clears quickly. We've got an important cricket match tomorrow against West Runton… you are coming to watch, darling?'

'What? Oh, yes.'

And then Posie stood stock still, elated as thunder threatened, not far off. She felt a little wild.

'I *adore* storms. If I could, I would bottle that smell. It's topping. I'd sell it. I'd call the perfume "Storm in My Soul" or "The Weather is Changing", or some such fluffy nonsense. But the scent, it would be exactly like *this*: a big blossoming bubble of danger. I'd wear it every day.'

And when she laughed after saying this, wondering if she had said too much, she met Harry's storm-reflected eyes, and felt alarmed to read there was nothing much there.

There was only a surprised blankness.

This much was confirmed by a parcel arriving at the Rectory the very next day, biked over by one of Marchpane & Marchpane's delivery boys.

On opening it, Posie was surprised to take delivery of a large, expensive bottle of scent.

It was Yardley's bestselling 'English Rose'. Accompanying this was a written note:

YESTERDAY YOU SAID YOU'D LIKE A NEW BOTTLE OF SCENT.
SEE YOU VERY SOON,

YOUR VERY BEST,
HARRY.

Posie was dumbfounded. She remembered her brother's unwelcome words: *He'll never understand you.*

Was Richard actually right?

She didn't know what to think or say. So she did the only thing possible. She decided to put it from her mind absolutely.

The bottle of scent was destined for Mrs Hickory as an early birthday present, and Harry never asked about it again.

Dates for the wedding were briefly discussed, and dresses sketched out by Posie and Hattie on the back of envelopes, but then, in August 1914, the Great War came along instead.

And it blew their tiny and half-comfortable world apart.

At first, it was only the men who wanted to enlist who did so: those bored Blakeney boys who had been hanging around and wanting more excitement.

Groups of pals and work colleagues, joining the same units, all went off together.

Perry Briskow enlisted in the early autumn of 1914, setting an 'example' to his men in the factory, scores of whom followed.

In the heady days of late 1914, as Posie rode her glorious new bicycle across the flatlands of Norfolk, from Blakeney to Holt and back again, snatching time with Harry when she could, riding out together when possible, the war all seemed so new and exciting that the prospect of getting hurt, or even dying, was as remote in Norfolk as the idea of Australia.

But soon place names which meant nothing started to mean a great deal: *Lorraine*, *Charleroi*, *the Marne*, *Mons*.

They were plastered across the front pages of newspapers, again and again. All of these were battles.

All battles fought but not really won.

Reports starting to circulate of British troops digging

in to the mud of France in tunnels, as winter came on, living in the mud like rats.

People started speaking in low whispers about 'secret' hospitals being set up in remote English country houses, and of vast numbers of boys being sent home injured.

There were reports of men dying like animals, and staggering casualties.

Men on leave in the Norfolk coastal villages returned home tight-lipped, dead-eyed, smoking incessantly, drinking more.

The dashing Perry Briskow, now a Captain, came home for the Christmas of 1914 and Posie hardly recognised him at a small reception held in his honour at Holly House; he scarcely seemed to know who anyone was, and his teeth chattered constantly in a face which was twisted in pain.

He shook Posie's hand, calling her 'Polly', and then 'Lily', and as his big capable wife Gwendoline propelled him about the green parlour, it was clear he couldn't focus, constantly looking over to the open doorway, as if on watch for a very late but still-expected guest.

His great purple eyes seemed to Posie like vast open doors to a private hell he could scarcely begin to describe.

Once, he looked over towards the fireplace, then spun around puzzled, frowning, addressing the company in a panic.

'Whose bally black dog is this? Who thought it was a good time to buy a wretched dog?'

But there was no dog anywhere, let alone in the empty grate.

Posie watched as Sir Peregrine stared gimlet-eyed about the room, his face with its rictus grin terrible to behold. There were no jokes about ghost dogs today: no confrontational 'WOOF WOOF.'

Instead, Wykham hurried over to Perry, as others stared, intrigued, in a stupor of frozen fright.

Wykham half-coughed with becoming humility: 'It's

my dog, sir. He escaped the kitchens. I'll get rid of him now, sir: you don't need to trouble yourself a jot more. Why don't I pour you another single malt? Warm the cockles, sir, eh?'

And Posie heard a deep half-strangled moan beside her, and she strained to catch Harry muttering: 'Oh by Gad, my poor brother. He's gone quite mad!' and when she touched Harry's arm briefly, she felt him shaking beneath his thick tweed.

Perhaps *not* quite the time to mention to Harry her interest in ghosts generally, or the possibility that Perry had actually seen the house phantom?

Because in Posie's heart of hearts she knew that Harry wouldn't have understood. There would have been that blankness again.

Better to be mad than to see a ghost.

Better to talk of cricket than the scent of a storm.

Posie had warmed to Wykham immensely at this party. He was obviously a soother, and truly kind, in a way that no-one else had dared to be.

Sir Peregrine seemed smaller than ever at that rare party.

He paid Posie almost no attention, staring at his assembled sons with narrowed eyes, as a shepherd might count his sheep before dusk.

Perry returned to France in January 1915, colourless as a wraith, and days later he was reported missing in action, just south of Verdun.

That big strong Adonis, gone.

During the Christmas holiday Joseph Briskow had also joined up. He enlisted as a medical surgeon, and he was sent immediately to Gallipoli.

No-one ever heard from him again, and it wasn't until later that year, in August, that a telegram arrived for Girvan confirming Joseph's death from sickness and infected wounds at Suvla Bay.

It seemed to Posie that whatever had irked Joseph, whatever secrets haunted him, he took them, unspilled, to his premature grave.

Geoffrey Briskow, the professional soldier, whom Posie was still to meet, was also posted to Gallipoli. However, news from him was always patchy, and it was understood he was heading up a team of Australian soldiers.

And while concern was high for loved ones on the front line, people at home were now fearful for their own lives, too.

Because the Great War had suddenly come to Norfolk itself.

In January 1915 some of the topmost coastal resorts and villages came under attack from German Zeppelin bombing raids, and the sheer awfulness of these night-time attacks caused anger, disruption, and real fear.

Johnny Briskow had not yet volunteered, perhaps more shocked by the death of Perry than he could say. Posie noticed on the rare occasions when she saw him that he joked less.

The bank he worked at in Sheringham was obliterated by the Zeppelin raids, and as the year rolled on he seemed to be heavily involved in the rebuilding of it.

But in December of 1915 he received his own compulsory call-up papers, and he bade farewell to his one-year-old daughter as the days started to lengthen out again.

He came home in February for a snatch, on leave, and, in truth, he seemed his usual old self, full of bluster, and sporting a fashionable new square moustache, but just a month later Harry drove over to the Rectory with the news that Johnny was dead; killed on the first day of the Battle of the Somme.

Johnny never got the news his wife, Kate, sent to him with a box of goodies; that they were expecting another child. The box was returned to her unopened, marked 'RETURN TO SENDER.'

This was very much a strange twilight time for Posie, during which she wasn't invited to Holly House once.

She was very conscious of the disapproval of the Coven towards her, and, with the three recent and tragic deaths, she was also conscious that this obviously wasn't a time to celebrate a wedding, despite an engagement which was stretching on, and on.

Nor did Posie know how the family were mourning their dead, if at all? With no identifiable bodies to be sent home, there could be no funerals.

There were announcements of the Briskow son's deaths, of course, in all the parish magazines and in the local Holt newspaper.

But these were for everyone, bland and official. *Necessary*.

At each death Posie sent a black deckle-edged card, expressing her and her family's condolences.

But only silence greeted her words.

Endless, pressing, meaningful silence.

She sometimes saw Girvan Briskow cycling about efficiently between the criss-crossing network of coastal villages, her black midwife's bag strapped to her basket, but Girvan was always, understandably, in a hurry, and only ever waved fleetingly, and with her eyes cast well down.

Once Posie spotted her with one of her father's curates, both on black bicycles, capes sweeping out behind them, but it had only been the curate who waved.

Sometimes Posie saw the manservant, Wykham, at the post office in Holt, straight and black-jacketed and very proper, collecting and carrying parcels to and from Holly House.

He would touch his hand to his black bowler hat, and nod seriously, but he never said anything more than the essentials: 'Good morning, Miss,' or 'Pleasant weather we are having, Miss…' or once, 'I wish you well, Miss.'

Once she saw Mrs Noakes, hurrying through the Market Square, her face set grimly and carrying shopping.

But of the others, of Sir Peregrine himself, there was nothing.

Harry told Posie not to worry: it was their 'way' of grieving. After the Great War things would be fine, easy. *Wonderful.*

And so Posie met Harry alone.

They drove in his car to the beaches of Holkham, and walked over sand dunes, and once they went to Norwich together and had tea. She watched him play cricket in a team increasingly made up of old men.

They cycled, and cycled.

Posie got involved locally in war work; local women's groups in villages she could get to easily on her Sunbeam, sending out packages to the troops: socks, chocolate, cigarettes. But it was bitty work, unsatisfactory.

Her pal Hattie had enrolled to re-train as a nurse. Hattie wanted to go out to the front line.

'Won't you join me, Posie? We could ask to be stationed together?'

'I'd come with you in a heartbeat, you know that. But I can't.'

'Harry? Mnnn. He *is* a darling. I wouldn't want to leave him either. Thank goodness for his bad eyesight, eh? You know he won't be called up because of that.'

It wasn't just leaving Harry. There was her difficult father, too.

After Hattie had left for her nurses training, then on to France, rather surprisingly without coming around to say goodbye, Posie looked about for more purposeful work closer to home.

Several munitions factories were advertising for paid women workers.

A filling factory just outside Norwich was advertising constantly; with board and meals provided, and jolly good pay.

Posie placed the adverts by her father's dinner plate in

the evenings, only to watch him pick the pages up silently, scrunching them into a ball, throwing them onto the fire.

The Reverend Parker was obstinate.

'That work is not safe.'

As it turned out, it was one of the best things the Reverend Parker had ever done for Posie, keeping her away from the poisons which were used by the unprotected munitions workers.

Almost everyone seemed to know a girl working in the factories who was sick: Harry spoke vividly of their old parlourmaid, Millie, who had left their service to work in a filling factory.

Now she was dying in a Norwich hospital, with bright yellow skin and her red hair turned the colour of a nightmarish primrose, with only old Wykham and Mrs Noakes coming in with a hamper of food every other Sunday, in rotation.

Apparently Millie was on a ward with other girls who were all in the same boat; they were being called 'Canary Girls' by the doctors, and their chances of survival were next to nothing.

But Harry himself was doing well.

He was now a partner in his law firm and the gold plaque outside his offices now read 'MARCHPANE & BRISKOW'.

He spoke of a future which seemed to Posie almost impossible, like a fairytale, in which his days were much the same as now, and in which Holt and Posie were his whole world. An empire.

'When my father is dead Holly House will be all mine, darling. Geoffrey will never return, mark my words; even if he *does* survive this war. We'll fill the place with children, darling: won't we? Lots.'

'Sounds marvellous. But perhaps we should set a date to get married first?'

Posie wagged her left-hand ring finger with its flash of shiny blue stone in the air, only half in jest.

'Mnnn. Rather boringly, my father doesn't seem in the mood somehow, ever since Johnny died. He was going to make a generous settlement for us; an allowance of money for our marriage. I was rather holding out for it. I'll pester him again, and if I haven't got anything firm from him by Christmas we'll just marry at your father's church in a quiet ceremony, anyhow. Your father's already given his blessing, after all.'

But had he? Had he, really?

And after this talk of marriage they made love for the first time.

It was in a candy-coloured beach hut which Harry rented for an afternoon at an off-season rate at Mundesley Beach. A mauve one.

He was considerate, assured, obviously practiced.

Afterwards he slept naked in her arms for hours and she got a pain in her back from the first cold drafts of September wind, rushing up at them through all the cracks in the floor, reminding them of winter.

He'd worn a fine, fine gold chain about his neck which Posie realised she'd never seen before on account of his clothes, and on the end of this chain was an unusual gold key, probably a charm rather than a real key: fine, flat, tiny, with small angel wings carved into the top.

It was a lovely thing. A secret thing, and Posie wondered if Harry would ever tell her about it.

Posie wondered if it had belonged to his mother, and it gave her a good feeling that Harry held onto his memories of his mother so strongly still.

The following Sunday Harry told her he had joined up, at his father's encouragement.

'He said I should do my part. Frankly I'm jolly surprised, given he's lost three of us already. But I doubt I'll be called up, darling. Not with my terrible eyesight. Don't worry. I've pretty much been assured of it. I'm not going anywhere.'

He certainly didn't expect to go near an active front.

However, two months later Harry's papers came, and Posie waved him off at Sheringham Station, a peculiar little clutch of fear pulling at her heart.

He was quite scared, she could see that, but there had been no talk of seeing any black dogs at Holly House, and for this Posie was peculiarly grateful.

The evening before he left Harry gave Posie a 'promise' ring, a gold band with little chips of diamond in it, forming a fancy curving line, like the sea.

He had bought it at the same time as the sapphire ring. It should have been the wedding ring.

'I'll come back for you, Posie,' Harry whispered.

They'd stolen a carefully-arranged hour together in Mrs Hickory's rather grotty and damp small apartment near the stable block at the back of the Rectory. It had been kind of her to be complicit in their affairs. She was out anyhow at choir practice, but she winked at Posie before going, saying she 'remembered what it was like to be young.'

The lovers lay together, close: skin sheeny, energy spent. Posie reached for the angel-wing key and touched it inquisitively, but Harry gently prised her fingers away.

'I'll tell you about this another time,' he said, sighing.

A late November frost moon was in the sky and Posie looked at it through the window which was smeary with condensation. She only half-heard what her fiancé was saying:

'I'll marry you soon. No waiting for anyone. Settlement or no settlement. And if anything happens to me, please know you were the most beautiful girl who ever came into my life. By Gad, I have such plans. Such plans.'

'Mnnn.'

They had one short 'leave' together, in April. It was snatched and unsatisfactory.

And then one month later Harry was dead.

Sir Peregrine had been dealt a full hand of sons, but now he was running on a definite losing streak.

* * * *

Four

After the telegram came with its news of Harry's death, out on the Messines Ridge, in the summer of 1917, Posie felt stunned.

His death threw her.

She moved as if sleep-walking, searching for a purpose.

Her father offered the briefest of regrets, before shutting himself in his study, ostensibly to 'write'.

Her brother, Richard, also out fighting on the Western Front, wrote to Posie expressing his condolences, but his telegram contained a kernel of his former disapproval:

Poor old Po,
Sorry for your loss. Grieve now for Harry, and then move on.

She cycled to Holly House, but it was in vain.

No-one was at home. Its long eye-like windows looked to be shuttered up.

What should she do?

What were the residents of Holly House up to? Had they all gone away?

In the months since Harry had left for war, Posie had had nothing at all to do with his family, and she'd kept herself busy: she was helping at the dairy in Blakeney, doing unpaid deliveries, and where, rather thrillingly, she had learnt to drive a motor-van, which she adored.

But what was her position as a not-quite-wife, anyhow?

She felt she should certainly try and pass on her personal condolences to Sir Peregrine, as a bare minimum.

Before Hattie Draper had departed so suddenly, she had always been Posie's main source of local gossip, and now Posie had to put feelers out elsewhere for news of Sir Peregrine and the Coven.

She went to Harry's place of work, where Harry's boss Regulus Marchpane, whom she'd never really spoken to before properly, was very welcoming, being both sorrowful and affectionate.

Posie couldn't help but notice that the shiny new gold plaque with the name 'MARCHPANE & BRISKOW' had already been unbolted from the wall and a grubby, empty space remained.

So much for dreams, Posie thought, half-bitterly, and yet half-amused.

Mr Marchpane brought Posie a cup of tea and opened a packet of Peek Frean biscuits.

He leant against his big old partner's desk, arms crossed around his wiry form, and he sighed deeply.

'What a bally old mess, eh, Miss Parker? Poor old you. And poor old Peregrine. I'm lucky I never married, never had children; I can't feel the loss. This war has a lot to answer for. You asked about Peregrine? Doesn't want to see a soul. Won't hear of it: won't even go to church, let alone organise memorials. Only Wykham, that faithful old bounder, is there to do his bidding, with Noakes. All the other servants are long gone of course.'

Regulus Marchpane had firmer news on the wives. He reported that Girvan Briskow was long gone too, nursing in a Casualty Clearing Station out on the Western Front.

Kate Briskow, now with two very small daughters in tow, had retreated to her parents' house in the relative safety of Scotland, while Gwendoline Briskow had moved down to London where she had been very active in aid work for children.

Regulus Marchpane munched on a biscuit thoughtfully.

'I heard that Gwendoline died a couple of weeks ago in a Zeppelin raid in central London; killed in broad daylight in a small school as she sorted out clothes for local children. It makes you wonder, doesn't it? What it's all *for*?'

'It does. And you, sir? I see you've taken down the new sign? Will you continue here alone? Or will one of your colleagues step in as partner, now Harry is gone?'

'I don't know what Harry told you, Miss Parker, but there were really just the two of us here, with my old secretary, Miss Pitts, and two boys who ran errands. And now even *they* are gone, off to the wretched war.'

Regulus looked a little shame-faced as he dusted his lap of crumbs.

'You asked about the office sign. I am truly sorry for your loss, Miss Parker, I am. And in his way Harry Briskow was an enthusiastic and very good lawyer, but I must admit I was never entirely happy with the partnership we'd set up together, but times were tight for me financially, and so I accepted his offer to come in on a half-share. I will be putting up my old sign again soon, without the 'Briskow' name, and then I can feel truly genuine again. If life has taught me one thing, Miss Parker, it is to be true to oneself. Compromise is never a good thing.'

Posie was confused at this odd snippet of explanation. 'Had Harry done something wrong, sir? Here? He'd let you down? You seem disapproving, somehow.'

'Gracious no, dear lady. As I said, Harry was an excellent lawyer.' Regulus lit a pipe already filled with tobacco, inhaled slowly.

'I know you want to do the right thing, Miss Parker, but walk away from here now, and go and live your life. Get a job, ladies *can* these days, can't they? If you need a reference I'll gladly supply one. There will be a big joint memorial service for Harry, and his brothers, along with all the other boys from this town who will never return home, when this war is done. *If* it is ever done… but hopefully you will be elsewhere when that service happens, enjoying yourself. We must look to the living, eh?'

Look to the living.

She could do that.

Time is precious.

But the scattered Briskow women with their meaningful occupations proved an inspiration to Posie, and she headed to her old haunt, the library Reading Room.

Posie scanned the newspapers desperately, trying to find a job in which she could make a difference. A real difference.

One advert stood out immediately, specifying the ability to drive as a necessity, and Posie jumped at the chance, applying immediately.

And so it was that Posie signed up for the Women's Ambulance Driving Corps.

The month-long training was in Norwich.

She packed up her holdall quietly and only told her father about the Driving Corps the day before she left.

Unsurprisingly, he was apoplectic with rage, blustering.

'Isn't it enough that your brother is out in that hell-hole? Besides which, you can't even drive!'

'I can, actually, Father. I've been driving for months.'

'So, you're lying now, too, eh? I'll call the Bishop: make him tell you to see sense.'

'The Bishop would tell me I'm right to be doing my duty, and anyhow, you wouldn't dare involve him in our family affairs, Father! They're too bally odd.'

'Watch your tongue, Rosemary Parker. And how exactly will you get to Norwich?'

'I've enough for the train fare. But I *do* need to pay for my digs while I'm there…'

'Forget it. You'll not get a penny from me.'

'Fine.'

And so Posie promptly packed up Harry's most precious gifts, including the Sunbeam, which she stashed in the Guard's carriage on the train.

As soon as she got to Norwich she found a pawn shop in Tombland and she sold the silver fox fur and the sapphire engagement ring and her lovely bike, and these things made her a good whack of money.

Funnily enough, she wasn't sad about selling anything, except the Sunbeam, which had represented a tiny slice of freedom at a time when it had been hard to come by.

Posie spent a month in the city, and didn't return to the Rectory once, although she sent postcards home, which all went unanswered. And then she was packed off to France.

And nothing would ever be the same again.

* * * *

Posie, in the here and now, was ready to leave the dim Temple Church.

She fished in her carpet bag and brought out her handkerchief to tidy her face, and at the same time she accidentally brought out the single sheet of newspaper which she had been meaning to read earlier, in the café.

The Norwich Mail.

A story about a Norfolk murder, wasn't it?

How funny that she had carried on thinking about Norfolk here.

She'd go and read it somewhere warm, in a few minutes, with a nice coffee and a piece of fruitcake.

Or a scone.

Before hauling herself up, she sat on for a moment longer on the hard pew, her hand tight against her belly, where butterflies danced.

Why had she really come here?

Because now she couldn't get Norfolk out of her head.

By Gad, she had hated that place at times while growing up. Had longed for the grit and warmth and noise and lights and all the glamour that a big city gave you, and for her that city had always been London.

And here she was.

Here she had insisted they stay, even after her marriage to Lovelace and after the babies had come, and even after the flat on Bury Place had turned out to be too cramped, too unsuitable.

She held steadfastly onto the dream of her flat, but there were times when she felt selfish.

There was no garden for the children at the Bloomsbury flat, for example, and both Phyllis and Kit Lovelace had developed persistent sticky, tarry coughs this winter, made worse by the green smog that settled over the city every night before supper; creeping in at the window-panes and under the thick velvet curtains.

The smell of the smog was awful; sulphurous, acrid at the back of your throat.

And thinking of smells, Posie was suddenly overwhelmed by a sharp, sudden wall of scent. It wasn't incense or candles though, or any church-related stink. But something musty, cloying; so intense it made you want to gag.

It was a Christmassy aroma of cinnamon, cloves and nutmeg.

But in a second it was gone again.

I'm being fanciful.

She thought keenly of the clean, kelp-scented air and blue skies of Blakeney. There were no smogs in Norfolk.

Perhaps she could organise a holiday up there?

Perhaps she'd call Scotland Yard and try and put a holiday in her husband's diary. Perhaps he needed to get away from distractions down here; away from women who wore amber-scented perfume?

Who knew where it might lead?

Richard Lovelace was desperate for another child, Posie knew that; even though he swore blind he was happy with their lot in life, he, an only child, and an orphan to boot, had always dreamed of a brood of children. Three was lovely, but even more would be better.

Perhaps they would get lucky again, as they had with Kit?

They could take a Norland Nanny with them, and maybe Masha the Russian Housekeeper?

Maybe there was a chance Posie could book an empty, off-season beach hut for an afternoon? Drag her husband inside. Pounce on him. *And if he was really lucky she might even…*

But someone broke into her thoughts, coughed politely. 'Er, hullo?'

A man's voice. Rich and low.

'Excuse me. Miss Parker, isn't it? The Reverend Henry Parker's daughter?'

She turned sharply, all thoughts of beach huts and marriage-saving sex quite disappeared.

A man was sitting along in the pew from her, nearest the aisle. He was a couple of years older than she was; washed-out, and bald-ish, with a round moon of a face atop a scraggy thin neck, with small eyes and prominent ears.

He was undoubtedly no oil painting. But he didn't need to be, because he had a uniform which spoke of reassurance.

He wore the clothes of an everyday priest; a black cassock and white priest's collar, although his clothes were filthy, covered in dried-on mud. Perhaps worse.

What on earth had he been doing? Mud larking?

He smelt of salt and sweat and old things, even from

this distance. *Had he been running?* He could have done with a good bath.

But his presence was calm, and he smiled. It was a very kindly smile, but it was also the smile of a preoccupied man.

For a moment Posie thought he might stretch out his hand to her, and she hoped rather that he wouldn't, as he had revoltingly filthy hands, with very muddy and unsavoury-looking fingernails, all torn off in places.

Was he an ardent gardener in his spare time?

Posie remembered that it was quite common with priests. Her own father had once had a fancy for roses, which grew badly on the salt-spewn coast.

'You might not remember me, Miss Parker…'

She *did*, but from where? From here?

She had the feeling the man had been important, or useful, or both, perhaps, for her father. But a long time ago.

Was this one of her now-dead father's students?

'You're…'

'Yes. I'm glad you recall.' He nodded eagerly. 'I'm Norbert Carpenter, Miss Parker. I last saw you at your father's funeral, in 1920. You remember, it was *I* who wrote to you at the end of 1917? Asking you to return to England?'

'Of course.'

It all came back to her in a flash, clear as a bell.

Posie owed this man much. Her father had owed him much more.

Of course she remembered Norbert Carpenter. Although age had not been kind to him. His skin was papery in the dim light, and his small eyes looked weary and watery. He was clearly in dire need of a holiday.

She stretched out her hand to be polite, pulling off her glove as she did so.

'Oh, I won't shake hands.' He grimaced and indicated his own hands, ruefully. 'I've been fighting against what feels like an entire forest of wood, and I still show the scars. Sometimes one should recognise one's limits.'

'Gardening? In London? Here, at the Temple?'

'Not here, no. But this is an important place for me, undoubtedly. It's where I met your father, you know. When I was looking for a job. He persuaded me to come up to Norfolk. As a curate. I never left... They were happy days. Such kindness.'

Had they been happy days? Had there been kindness?

Posie tried not to blush. Her father and her brother had both had acid tongues, and dark, dark senses of humour. Combined, it had sometimes been a bit much. They were the type of men to pounce on weakness and hold it up and laugh about it.

She recalled now with shame how her father and her brother used to laugh mercilessly about this man, Norbert Carpenter. How they would mimic his rather fruity old-fashioned voice; make fun of his odd looks; scoff at his unstable health.

Ah, yes. His health.

His health kept him out of the Great War.

Carpenter had been a man who was often sick with colds and sniffles, and he'd had problems breathing from the moment he arrived in Blakeney. There had been difficulties with various Norfolk flowers and grains and scents.

He came out in rashes easily; broke out in weals on eating a smidgen of the wrong thing.

Norbert Carpenter was famous in the parishes for having a pre-written list of items he could *not* eat, which he'd hand to parishioners who might be kind enough to be hosting him for a Sunday dinner.

But her father, despite making fun of Norbert, had been losing his grip on both his mind and his benefice, and had come to rely very heavily on Norbert. Especially in the last year of the war.

The curate had been a mainstay, and by the end, a crutch.

Norbert had managed the five churches with a small team of other, younger curates, and he'd understood instinctively the juggling act of how to keep all the services running seamlessly and profitably, while keeping up the fiction that Posie's father was still the one who was still very much in charge.

He'd even written the Reverend Parker's sermons for him.

Norbert had been a familiar and slightly comic sight in Blakeney, haring about on a bicycle borrowed from his digs above a pub, cassock flying, always with a wide-brimmed canvas hat in summer, and what looked like a badly-knitted balaclava in winter.

Mr Minks, Posie's father's Siamese cat, particularly hated Norbert, and would pounce on him with an unusual level of maliciousness whenever Norbert arrived for his weekly briefings, which Posie's father used to find quite funny.

Norbert had been allergic to the cat anyway, coughing and sniffing and rubbing at his eyes, and so these encounters were never particularly happy ones for him.

When Posie left for France in 1917 her father had slid into an even more serious level of decline and then, it seemed, Norbert Carpenter had really come into his own.

He'd taken care of the Reverend Parker like the son he *did* have, but who was absent.

And when Posie's own brother had been reported as missing in action at Cambrai, and later, confirmed dead, Norbert had tried to rally the Reverend Parker, who took to his bed and never got out of it again.

His own attempts to help the Reverend Parker having failed, eventually Norbert had written to Posie asking for help, and she had come immediately.

He'd transferred to King's Lynn Minster shortly afterwards, and had done well at the Cathedral there, and she knew he had later been given his own benefice because he had told her so at her father's funeral.

He'd done rather well.

'Where are you based now, Reverend Carpenter?'

'Blakeney, actually.' He twisted his hands. 'Sometimes things come full circle.'

They gazed at each other for a moment, and Posie stared into the watery grey eyes of the man next to her. In her mind's eye she had remembered his eyes as a vivid blue, the only feature about the poor man which had been memorable.

But it turned out that she had remembered him wrong.

Posie grinned. 'You went back? How lovely. I haven't been in years, but funnily enough I was just sitting here contemplating doing exactly that... Are you at my father's old Rectory? Did you marry? Oh, listen to me. So nosy. Forgive me. And forgive my impertinent questions!'

Carpenter laughed easily.

'I know you're a detective, Miss Parker, and questions are your way of making a living. You were always a curious girl; the sort people felt they could talk to. The sort people would try and seek out. I've followed your cases, you know. Congratulations. You're famous! I'm glad you got away. You were too full of life to be contained by so small a place.'

He didn't add anything like '*Your father would be proud of you*' because they both knew that wouldn't be true.

Instead, he replied to Posie's cheeky question thoughtfully, slowly: 'I have not married, no, although I must confess it is not for want of trying. And as for your father's Rectory, it has been sold, Miss Parker. A few years ago. It is being changed, like everything. It will become a bed-and-breakfast, I understand. They are building a new Rectory, but meantime, I stay where I can. I'm at the big house in Holt. You know it, I think; Holly House?'

Posie felt the acid rise in her throat. She didn't reply.

Because the way he had said '*You know it,*' made her

think he knew all about Harry Briskow and the former occupants of the house.

But before Posie could quiz him further, she saw how Norbert was looking at the sheet of newspaper still by her side on the pew.

'Oh!' he exclaimed, almost in relief. 'You've read that, Miss Parker? Well, that certainly makes things easier for me…'

'Sorry? Oh, no. I haven't read it yet.'

She picked the newsprint up. 'Wait up. What's it about? Give me a minute.'

But suddenly the portly young man with the moustache – who must be the resident choirmaster – rushed down the aisle, with many, many musical scores heaped uncomfortably highly in his arms, held in place by his chin.

As he passed them he frowned, then stopped abruptly next to Norbert, sniffing the air, his small rather red mouth pursed up uncomfortably.

'I say, sir,' said Norbert Carpenter to the man. 'You're Mr Thalben-Ball, I believe? If so then I have heard such wondrous things about your music: you're quite renowned. I have a HMV recording from here, actually: your quite wonderful 'Hear My Prayer' by Mendelssohn. I was listening to it only yesterday. Goodness, but it would be a treat to get along to one of your concerts for real! It really would, if travel here was a little easier. When is your next concert?'

But the choirmaster ignored Carpenter, and stared very hard from the priest to Posie, and back again, suspiciously.

It was very rude, even if the Reverend Carpenter *did* smell.

Or perhaps Mr Thalben-Ball had thought it was Posie who niffed a bit?

Or, and Posie felt her face flush red at this even worse thought, perhaps he thought she and Carpenter were up to something fishy, despite their sitting so far apart?

A bit like the German couple?

Heaven forbid.

But the man seemed to recover himself very slightly, and he smiled a little distractedly. 'I must apologise to you; we've had problems all morning with the drains here. It ruined choir practice and it seems to be lingering on. I hope it hasn't ruined your visit here, and I must assure you it is certainly being dealt with.'

Drains?

Posie felt immediately bad for having assumed it was Norbert who stank so strangely.

'That's Mr Thalben-Ball,' hissed Norbert as the man moved off, although Norbert's face was crestfallen. 'He's the most wonderful choirmaster and organist this church has ever had. A virtuoso, I read. They say he can hear a voice like no other can. I suppose he's in his own little musical world though, composing something, so he doesn't like to chat about music to admirers like me. Oh, well...'

He indicated to the paper in Posie's hands. '*Do* read that article, Miss Parker. My coming here will be very much explained by it.'

Posie checked the date again. The page from *The Norwich Mail* had been published one week earlier. Norbert edged closer towards Posie and the scent from earlier wafted from him strongly. Christmas spices again.

It seemed to emanate from him, whatever the choirmaster had said about drains.

What the dickens was it? Some strange and natural remedy for one of the Reverend Carpenter's ailments, she supposed.

But Posie's worry about Norbert's strange odour instantly evaporated when she read the headline.

As she read, a tight hand of fear clamped at her throat.

She read it again, and again.

And it didn't get any better with the re-reading.

NORFOLK MURDER OF RECLUSIVE HOLT BUSINESSMAN NOW SOLVED!

As reported in this newspaper last week, local magnate Sir Peregrine Briskow, 75 years old, of Holly House, Holt, was found murdered in cold blood just over a week ago.

He was shot in the chest.

Police had wondered on initial investigation if the murder was a by-product of a bungled burglary, as several precious items were reported as missing: jewellery, a fob-watch, Treasury notes.

However, police are now agreed that one of the residents of the house, a Mrs Girvan Briskow, 35 years old and the widow of Dr Joseph Briskow, acted deliberately in the cold-blooded murder of her father-in-law.

Evidence points this way and Mrs Briskow has been arrested and will be tried for the murder in a special session court at the Norwich Assizes in one weeks' time, starting on 15TH FEBRUARY.

The Judge who will hear the case is the infamous Lord Justice 'END OF THE ROAD' Roade. It seems a virtual certainty that Mrs Briskow will hang.

Police Inspector William 'Vinny' Vin

of the Holt Constabulary was reported as saying: 'This is a sad day for Holt residents. Who can you trust if not your own family? We are happy, however, that justice has been served, and will be served, in this very tragic case.'

We will continue to bring you the news on future developments.

'Oh, dear God.'

Posie stood up, and Norbert Carpenter did so too. He was gazing at her fixedly.

'I should go there,' said Posie. 'To Holt. Now.'

He nodded, not smiling at all, and they were both out in the aisle, walking quickly. Almost marching. Side by side, the newspaper still in Posie's hand.

'Why didn't you call me before?' asked Posie, urgently, and slightly afraid, although she didn't exactly know why.

'My number at the agency is on the main exchange. More time is always better. Oh! But you *did* call me!'

The realisation hit her suddenly.

Posie remembered the scrappy note from Suzannah about a man calling, over and over. Due to the lack of date supplied Posie had presumed the note was of today's date, but that was to credit Suzannah with a certain degree of logic she probably didn't have. The note could easily have been from anytime this week, but only 'remembered' or 'discovered' today.

'You telephoned?'

'Well, in truth I only managed to get here today.'

Posie then remembered the page of newspaper in its plain envelope, and the footsteps she had heard earlier, chasing her, and the man's voice calling her name.

'You went to my agency, where you dropped the

newspaper page, and then you waited for me, and followed me here?'

'I did try to track you down, yes… it was hard going, actually.'

'You mean my bally awful Secretary? I'm really so sorry.'

'I was lucky to find you here,' he said humbly. 'It's a place which pulls at both of us strongly, obviously. I find it almost unbelievable how strong the pull of a heart can be! But there *is* time, isn't there? In the normal course of things? It says in the newspaper that the case won't be heard until next week.'

'Monday,' corrected Posie snappily, more harshly than she'd meant to.

'It's in three days. And nothing about this case will be normal. This is Lord Justice Roade we're talking about. He's a devil of a man. The devil incarnate, actually.'

She supposed it was the involvement of this particular individual, famous as a 'hanging' Judge, and with whom she had had some dealings in the past, which made her want to act quickly and rush about.

'Hold on a minute, Reverend Carpenter.'

They stopped by the effigies of the Knights, and Posie wondered quite why it was that she cared so much.

All of this, Norfolk, Holly House, the Briskows, were so far removed from the person she had become, from where she was *now*, that, until today, she had barely thought of them at all.

In fact, she had supposed old Sir Peregrine, old 'Boots', had died already.

And when she had left Norfolk finally and forever, in 1921, before coming to London to start up her Detective Agency, she hadn't given Sir Peregrine a second thought. Hadn't given Harry a second thought either.

Her face flushed red again.

So old 'Boots' had been murdered? And the very unfriendly Girvan was still around?

How bizarre.

Posie had never seen her in the intervening years. Girvan hadn't exactly been a friend, had she?

She'd supposed Girvan, if she'd thought of her at all, had either died in the Great War, much like Hattie had done, out in a Clearing Station somewhere, or else left for adventures new. Perhaps gone back to Northern Ireland?

So why on earth had Girvan been in Holt, at Holly House, two weeks ago anyhow?

Had Girvan been visiting there? Staying?

Did she live there? Had she lived there all along?

Posie had never wanted to go back to Norfolk since her father died. And now, today, here in this church, by some odd coincidence, her thoughts and memories had raised ghosts who had now been presented to her in a very real way in the bold print of a newspaper article. People who had now undergone a personal tragedy; a new horror.

The coincidence of this unsettled her slightly.

'I take it you want me to investigate, sir, although you haven't said as much? I suppose you think Girvan Briskow is wronged?'

'She is my parishioner,' Norbert replied softly. 'I know she has a very good heart. I cannot believe she is capable of this.'

'And if she *is*?' Posie said insistently.

'God is merciful,' the Priest said, doggedly. 'He sees everything. Besides, sometimes things are not as they first seem.'

Suddenly a door behind the effigies of the Knights Templar was thrown back on its hinges with a loud bang, revealing a room beyond full of clutter. Posie saw a flash of blue, of green.

But at this very moment the roar of an organ started up overhead, the chords pounding. Mr Thalben-Ball was warming up.

Posie and Norbert Carpenter were barely paying

attention to the music though. They were riveted by what was happening right in front of their eyes. The door by the effigies was held open as far as it would go, by a young clergyman; pious, disapproving.

'Charlatans! Liars! Get out,' the young priest barked sanctimoniously. 'This is a house of God, not a den of vice. What were you *thinking*?'

From the room came the German couple, rather shame-faced, but also rather radiant, somehow. The girl was squirting herself with a strong musky perfume.

The young priest tutted loudly and the door slammed closed again.

Posie watched as the couple moved apart, with the girl hurrying past them, heading for the exit alone, attaching what looked like a red rosette to her coat.

The blonde man hung back, peering at some postcards, putting some money in a collection tin.

After a couple of minutes, the man went out, too.

Posie frowned.

'As I said, Miss Parker. Sometimes things are not as they seem.'

Norbert Carpenter laughed with a spark of enjoyment. 'I see some things escape you, Miss Parker. Even a detective can miss clues.'

'What did I miss?' She felt wrong-footed, and besides, there was something else which was now pulling at her thoughts, very insistently.

Norbert nodded towards the exit. 'I got here after you, remember? There was a big German tourist party outside, in the precincts, due to go for an early lunch. But they had lost two of their number: the German female translator and one young husband. After a little bit of half-hearted searching, and discussion, which I overheard, the English Tour Guide decided the group should go for their planned lunch anyhow and loop back here afterwards. I think that boy's wife is much, much older than him. Rich, by the look of her. Well, perhaps both husband and wife know how to keep each other happy… perhaps by finding pleasure elsewhere?'

'Gracious. But you're a priest, you're not supposed to support the unorthodox view, are you?'

'Who are we to judge? Love and desire are sometimes found in the oddest of places.' Norbert shrugged ruefully. 'But now I really must go.'

'Are the trains still very bad to Norfolk? You said the journey here was difficult?'

'The trains are beyond dreadful,' he smiled, cocking his head to one side. 'Whichever way you go it takes an age. I'm just so glad I tracked you down: I'm relieved you've agreed to take this on. It's jolly good of you.'

Foolhardy, rather.

Posie chewed at her lip. She was unsure as yet of her exact arrangements. 'I'll see you up there?'

'You will. Certainly. I'll head back now.'

'Fine.'

And then he was gone, rustling, clipping along, hopefully taking his strange range of smells away with him.

But Posie was banging on the wooden door to the room the secret lovers had been thrown out of.

She was almost trembling with excitement.

After a minute or so a bolt was drawn back and the door slid open. The young priest from before looked out suspiciously.

'Yes?'

Posie craned her neck and looked in behind him. She pointed into the room, realising she was still holding the folded sheet of newspaper.

'Can I help you, Madam?'

The room was cavernous, lit with those peculiar little barred windows you often find in church vestries, causing a subterranean, bottom-of-the-sea glow to penetrate.

Even with this strange light you could see the place was a glorified cupboard for jumble, for church bric-a-brac which was no longer needed, but had yet to be properly sorted. A sort of purgatory for church paraphernalia.

Posie had seen something here which pulled at her heart, at her very being. Perhaps it meant more to her even than Norbert Carpenter's appearance today.

She had seen a crumple of green velvet; a golden halo; blue-satin arms stretched out in endless, eternal supplication.

'Could I…?' Posie pushed past the young man, emboldened by her quest.

They were part of a broken mass on the floor, underneath old baskets for flowers and cracked vases and prayer cushions which had become unravelled. The smell was damp but the appeal was as strong as ever.

'I say, Madam!'

Posie bent down, and there was Mary, on the floor. Posie pushed a pile of mildewy hymnbooks out of the way.

The mother of God was still eerily lifelike, her glassy blue eyes fixed on the floor, but her head had been cracked open, all at the back, like an eggshell, and straw stuffing was leaking out.

A huge crack fissured the forehead down to her nose.

'Oh!'

Posie bent down, as reverently as she had when she was a child.

The baby Jesus was still intact, but his human-hair was motheaten and shabby. The paint of his plaster lips was flaking away in red blisters. The halo did not glow at all.

The priest hovered uncomfortably.

'You're here for *them*, Madam?'

Posie looked up, confused. 'Well…'

I was, once.

'Only, we've been waiting for them to be picked up for ages. Lingered here for years. Pile of old rubbish, if you ask me. The choirmaster told me to wait in here with them; they've been asked for, requested. A collector, apparently. Coming here today. That's why I let that other couple in:

these models were made in Germany, hundreds of years ago, and I thought that as they were German, they would be the right people. How wrong I was! They played me for a fool. I left them alone for only five minutes.'

He screwed up his face in disgust. 'Charlatans, both of them. But you, Madam, are *you* the collector? You seem to know the figures... You obviously appreciate them.'

Posie had put out her hand to Mary's face and her dry fingers with their silver-tipped nails hovered above the fragile plaster cheek.

But she was interrupted by the young clergyman again.

'I say, Madam. I *do* apologise. Can you smell that dreadful smell? I do hope it's not coming from the figures, and it doesn't put you off buying them? It smells like mulled wine, gone off. Choirmaster thinks it's a drain, and plumbers are coming. I'd better go and see if they've arrived.'

And in that brief moment alone, Posie pulled her hand back.

She didn't really need to know if Mary felt warm to the touch.

Some mysteries were worth holding on to, even when reduced to rubbish, down in tatters on a cold stone floor.

****

PART TWO
Norfolk
(February 12 and 13, 1926)

Five

Posie was at Liverpool Street Station, waiting for a boy on a bike.

Standing with her small holdall at her feet, Posie blew on her icy hands.

She'd just made three telephone calls from a booth, and had had success with all of them, and so far, apart from this lad's lateness, everything was going to plan. But he'd better hurry, because her train for Norwich, from where she needed a connection through to Holt, was leaving in ten minutes.

Having left the Temple Church, she'd hailed a motor-taxi and packed a small bag of clothes at home in her flat, and kissed baby Kit and little Katie goodbye, before rushing on through to New Scotland Yard.

She'd stormed up the six flights of circular stone stairs to her husband's massive office on the very top floor of the red-bricked building, and flung open the door.

Since she hadn't called ahead, she wasn't quite sure what she had expected to find. However, it certainly hadn't been the boring sight of her husband, the Chief Commissioner, at the head of a long sheeny wooden table, snapping out instructions to his fleet of Inspectors.

There wasn't a single woman in sight.

Lovelace had stood up immediately, the colour draining from his face.

He cleared the room with one flick of his hand, and his men had gathered up papers and pens and half-burning cigarettes all in a rush, clearing out respectfully, as if there had been a death.

Well, there had.

'What is it, Posie?'

Richard faced her squarely, head back, shoulders braced, very upright.

'Tell me quickly, darling. One of the children?'

'The children are fine, but I need your help,' she'd replied, a little guilty at his obvious panic. 'With a small case. I'm going to Norfolk. Immediately. The one o'clock train.'

'WHAT? Is that *it*? I thought the worst! By Gad! What were you thinking? A telephone call would have sufficed, surely?'

Lovelace raged at her, throwing himself into his desk-chair with a roar like a wounded lion.

Eventually he had calmed down, and going through the rigmarole of lighting up his cigarette seemed to help.

She sketched out the details of the case. 'I need the police case notes,' she had said confidently. 'It's an Inspector Vin in charge.'

Her husband had groaned at the name. 'He's a bally menace!' he snapped. 'I've had dealings with him, years back. At Bury St Edmunds. Useless, conceited, slimy fella. He's been moved all over the place and it seems he's currently a big fish in a very little pond. Holt? Pah! You say Justice Roade is trying this one? Well, the woman is already dead, then, isn't she?'

He'd sighed. Said he'd like to help but that Holt, and Norfolk generally, were not Scotland Yard's remit.

Lovelace then explained that the best to be hoped for was that, as per usual custom, the police case notes were all prepared and still sitting in their pink-ribboned bundle at the High Court here in London, waiting for the Judge to collect them before he travelled north on the way to the trial.

'If Roade has already picked them up, there's nothing we can do.'

Richard had sighed wearily: 'If they *are* there, I'll get a lad to pick them up, and you can take them on with you, Posie. But you *must* make sure they get dropped off and registered at Norwich Court, so you'll have to read them on the train and make your own notes. I'll make up some fiction to Judge Roades about how the police case notes have been sent on in error; in a burst of over-efficiency. *As if!* I don't much like it, I must confess, sweetheart. It's all highly irregular, of course.'

He'd then stood, smoking by the window, gazing out at the blue pearly sky shot through with puffs of white cloud, at the silver River Thames glittering snake-like below; the endless cars and horses and people swarming along the Embankment.

He didn't turn, but he spoke to Posie's reflection in the glass, through clouds of his smoke.

'I'd take you out for lunch, darling, but I realise you need to go. Home territory, eh? This case? That's your old stomping ground, isn't it? Holt?'

'Yes and no. My father was the Rector at Blakeney, so near enough.'

'You know the people involved in this case?'

'By reputation only.'

'I see. But it's important to you?'

'Yes.'

'I read about this, in the internal police national crime report, although it hasn't yet made the national press. Not yet, anyhow. It *will*, if Roade is involved, and if this woman they've got in jail is even remotely good-looking. But it seemed a fishy sort of case to me. A bungled burglary?

A woman found guilty a couple of days after the crime? Promise me you'll take care, my love.'

He had coughed, embarrassed. Lowered his voice.

'I'm sorry I left in a mad bally dash this morning, Posie. I do realise I've had a lot on my mind lately, but believe me when I tell you that I was trying to organise something special for *you*. A trip away, and a gift. I'd ordered something I wanted to pick up before work today: a Valentine's gift, actually. I suppose I won't even see you now on Valentine's Day? And just so you know, I'd have loved to have stayed with you in bed this morning; with you in just that darn tiny bit of lace wrapping...'

He'd stubbed out his cigarette, turned, grinned wolfishly at her, almost growled: 'I suppose you don't have time now? I *could* lock the door?'

'No,' replied Posie firmly, and anyhow, just at that moment Sergeant Fox had stuck his head around the door. He was doing his Inspectors exams and needed Lovelace to sign a form.

'Lots of late nights then, Sergeant?' Posie asked.

He'd half-groaned. 'You bet, Miss.'

But here, now, at Liverpool Street, standing with one foot on the first-class train step, and with porters and conductors rushing about impatiently, she finally saw a young lad come hurtling down the platform, barely visible among the huge puffs of engine smoke.

He held a brown package tied up with pink ribbon and was waving it above his head dramatically.

Posie held out her arms for it as if he might throw it for her to catch. It seemed in that moment to be unbearably precious.

Safely received, and ensconced in the comfort of her train carriage and with a three-hour journey to kill, Posie read the police case notes slowly.

She wrote everything down, word for word, so she had a copy, and then she put all the facts together in one place, on one page, so she had her own summary.

It was a horrid little tale.
Her summary was as follows:

1. The Murder:

On Friday 29th January, 1926, at 3.30 pm, the Manservant of the Briskow family, Jeremy Wykham, called the police to come to Holly House, Holt.

He, together with one Housekeeper, Mrs Nora Noakes, are the only servants in the place.

He had returned from his usual weekly trip to the bank in town (an errand he always runs for his Master, Sir Peregrine, at the same time every single Friday. Every week he deposits Treasury notes at the bank, mainly takings from the family factory, and then completes anything else which Sir Peregrine may ask him to do).

Wykham reported that his Master was dead, shot twice: once in the head and once in the chest.

Sir Peregrine was collapsed on the floor of his study, in front of the fireplace.

The desk was in disarray, with evidence of a thorough search of the whole place having been attempted. Intruders had obviously got in.

A tentative record of death by murder or manslaughter by persons unknown was recorded by Inspector Vin, and then the sons, Geoffrey and Miles, who live at the property, later confirmed that various items had gone missing.

These items were: one hundred pounds in Treasury notes (the rest having been taken to the bank that day by Wykham), a gold fob-watch which had belonged to the victim's late wife, and a small black-diamond set brooch, also belonging to the late Emily Briskow.

The Pathologist's report indicates that death occurred

around 2pm on the day in question; cause of death being two gunshots, administered at close range.

2. The People Staying in the House:

SERVANTS

MR WYKHAM, in a self-contained flatlet on the top floor, and MRS NORA NOAKES, the Housekeeper, also on the top floor. Mr Wykham and Mrs Noakes, a widow, are sister and brother. Both are childless and unmarried.

THE SONS

The two surviving Briskow sons have a bedroom apiece on the third floor, although only MAJOR GEOFFREY BRISKOW, recently returned from India, is a permanent resident. He is almost certainly an alcoholic, and currently unemployed. Referred to in the police case notes as a 'bounder'. He had had 'words' with his father recently about taking over the running of the family boot factory, which he wanted, and which his father was set against. Sir Peregrine has a local man, Spears, in place at the factory. Spears oversees everything in Sheringham and has done so since the Great War, replacing Perry Briskow Junior from 1915 onwards. It seems Mr Spears is highly efficient and Sir Peregrine did not want to lose him.

Geoffrey's brother MILES BRISKOW is a Boarding Master at the local prep school, and usually only stays at Holly House one or two nights per week.

Both men were out when the body was discovered; Geoffrey was playing golf, and Miles was teaching.

OTHERS

A suite is laid out on the third floor for MRS GIRVAN BRISKOW, widow of the late Dr Joseph Briskow. She is much involved in charity work for women and has set up a couple of residential 'colleges' for destitute or socially excluded teenage girls in Belfast, and Mrs Briskow keeps an interest in these although does not need to be resident there for them to run efficiently. She had been at Holly House since before Christmas and was not planning on leaving soon. She has not confirmed where she was exactly at the time of death.

THE VICTIM

SIR PEREGRINE BRISKOW lived mostly in his downstairs study, where meals were brought to him by Wykham and where a bed was kept made up.

He was very infirm but his senses were alert, and it was understood and accepted by all the family that he had amended his Will to make provision for Mrs Girvan Briskow's share of the Briskow fortune to pass to her projects for girls, rather than to her personally.

At 5.00 pm, after the body had been removed, a cursory police search of the house was conducted. The following day a Forensics team from Norwich came in and the missing items were recovered from Girvan Briskow's bedroom. A Mauser C96 gun was recovered from the toilet cistern on the third floor, and this was later confirmed as containing bullets which were a match to that extracted from the chest cavity.

Two days later, following the results of these tests, and following confirmation that the Mauser C96 in question had been the wartime pistol of her late husband, Dr Joseph Briskow, Mrs Briskow was arrested, and underwent questioning which has proved inconclusive, although the evidence found indicates her guilt.

She will not confirm where she was or who she was with at the time of Sir Peregrine's death.

She has been in Holt Police Station ever since, in the holding jail there.

(The funeral of Sir Peregrine will take place next week.)

Posie tried to imagine it all.

A familiar house, but the years had passed and things must have changed. A much-reduced staff, for one thing. No more parlour maids.

Two brothers she had never met before.

She tried to imagine Sir Peregrine's study; she had been in there once. Harry's father had decided to show her a photograph of his dead wife, and it resided on his desk. Emily Briskow: she of the trim figure.

'Here, girl.'

Posie had been passed a blurry photograph of a woman with large frightened eyes and a face like beautiful Perry's, looking squeezed to death in a tight-looking corset.

Sir Peregrine had smoked his pipe in front of Posie, clearing out the bowl and filling it himself with an easy, practiced movement of the left hand, studying Posie's face as if for some sign of approval.

'She was beautiful, sir.'

'Wasn't she just?'

The study had been dark red, very much curtained, and big, warm tapestry rugs covered the floor and even some walls. It was cosy in a way the rest of the house was not.

The long, long windows had the same carved wooden original seats built into them, like the rest of the formal rooms in the house, and Posie remembered a fire crackling in the grate.

Changing at Norwich now, making sure to deposit the police case notes at the Court, and getting an official stamp to prove she had done so, Posie took another train which ran northwards then followed the jagged line of the coast past Cromer.

She stood at the carriage window peering out. The light was silvery, and it matched her clothes.

She saw the golden beaches flash past in a blur and the pier at Cromer where she had once eaten toffee apples with Harry; where they had seen an afternoon Variety Performance in the small theatre at the end of the pier; where they had shared a daring pint of bitter and held hands.

The innocence of the days before the mauve beach hut.

She had been worried about how she would feel being back here in Norfolk, but what she found was that she felt nothing.

Nothing apart from the sudden jolts of nausea from the moving carriage, and the sudden strong stink of the spice smell which would rush at her occasionally.

Really nothing.

At Holt Station she made her way to the Feathers Hotel on the Market Square, her old meeting-place for coffee with Hattie, which she had booked from the telephone booth when leaving London.

Up in her small attic room she ordered Earl Grey tea and changed into a set of sensible black woollen clothes she had hurriedly packed in London.

Funeral clothes, although as yet there was no funeral.

The clothes she had packed were warm, which was important. Up here the winds blew strong and she remembered how February and March had often been the months which had brought snow and big chilling freezes; snow blown over the rushy flatlands, icing up the Broads and the canals. She remembered how sometimes the waves were turned to salty blocks of ice on the beaches. Used as she was to the warmer climes of London she had come well prepared.

Posie reapplied her lipstick, a very vivid red, perhaps in remembrance of long-dead Hattie, and she added a dash of black kohl and lashings of mascara.

There.

She had a pair of her best and most expensive sapphire and diamond drop earrings with her and she added them quickly.

They had been a present from Rufus Cardigeon and his wife Dolly, back in the days before Dolly had gone missing, vanished forever. Dolly had been Posie's best friend, and Posie still held her in her heart, and the earrings had always proved lucky.

Having read over her summary page one final time, she folded the sheet of newsprint which Norbert Carpenter had given her earlier that morning, and placed it safely inside her silver notebook, and then all of this was placed in her old trusty carpet bag.

She went to the small reception and tried to place a call, to inform Richard that she had arrived, but the telephone at both his work and at their Bury Place flat just rang out, unanswered.

She wanted to place a call to Norbert Carpenter, too, as she was unsure where she should be meeting him, and now she was actually here she felt a bit of a fool.

What was it they had agreed, exactly?

He'd told her the Blakeney Rectory was no longer in use, and she'd thought he'd said he was at Holly House, but from the police reports he was not listed as a resident, so perhaps she had misunderstood? She'd hoped to meet and to make a plan, move forward together.

But Posie was used to working alone and she decided to forge ahead anyhow.

It was past tea-time when she reached the police station on the Market Square, opposite her hotel.

It was her first port of call for the evening, and she immediately saw that they had been expecting her.

Through the big sashed window of the street Posie saw that Inspector Vin was standing, one hand on his hip, casually leaning against the wooden reception counter, smoking a cigarette, his long horse-like face green-tinged below the electric lights.

He had greasy strands of black hair which he pushed back across a bald pate from time to time. His clothes, a plain flannel suit in chocolate, were immaculate and cut to flatter his lean, lithe figure. He obviously saw himself as a bit of a looker.

Posie had telephoned from Liverpool Street, explaining she was an old friend of the accused. She had also thrown in that she was married to Richard Lovelace.

Sometimes it didn't hurt to pull rank.

Inspector Vin gave Posie a toothy grin as she approached: 'A pleasure, Mrs Lovelace, a pleasure. *Do* remember me to the Chief Commissioner, won't you? Not like town, eh, is it, here? But we manage. We jolly along.'

Inspector Vin was originally a cockney, and he obviously missed the bright lights of London, and the busy East End, which had once been his life-blood.

He was friendly, over the top, enquiring about Posie's journey, almost bowling her along the little corridor with its painted-white brick walls and its familiar tang of institutional bleach and all the other awful smells underneath which it was trying to cover up.

The door to the interview room was propped open, and a metal teapot and a plate of newly-opened custard creams were already sitting on the table. Vin had obviously pushed the boat out for her tonight.

'You sit 'ere, Mrs Lovelace. The prisoner will be along in a minute.' Vin threw himself down – rather heavily for such a lithe man – into the wooden seat beside her.

Posie waited nervously, and to avoid small talk she took the biscuits, eating several rather hurriedly. She had her silver notebook out in front of her, ready, but she was still eating when Girvan Briskow was brought in by a Duty Sergeant, who positioned himself over by the door.

The woman, older than Posie by just a smidgen, was in handcuffs and a dirty old striped nightdress with long sleeves, which had obviously seen better days, but which was completely unsuitable for a Norfolk winter. Girvan had no shoes or stockings on, only wooden clog-like shoes and bare legs and feet. Her skin was blue with cold.

She had seemed small before, all those years ago, but now she appeared minute. Shrunken.

The black hair which had been up in a bun all those years before was now cropped to chin length, and a short, brutal fringe was cut high above her dark, intelligent eyes. She was still beautiful, but it was a haggard beauty, a beauty worn thin.

Girvan was devoid of her black spinel ring, the big house, the husband, the clothes, the prestige, which meant the roles of Girvan and Posie, compared to that bizarre tea party in the horrible green parlour all those years before, were now reversed.

And yet the will of the woman in front of Posie sparkled nonetheless. Girvan had a hauteur all of her own, and the way she conducted herself was like that of an angry dragon who is trapped, waiting to die.

'Posie Parker?' the woman whispered.

'Can it be? Little Posie Parker? After all this time?'

Girvan was defensive: 'You've done alright, Posie, haven't you? I must be honest and tell you you're actually quite beautiful now. And I see you've swapped Harry's Norfolk jewels for something fancier, eh? Those diamond earrings, oh my! They look like real Cartier. Aren't you just the ticket. Aren't you some fancy Private Detective now? Famous, by all accounts? So you must be catchin' killers all the time. Why are you here? The police have already caught me! Or are you here to gloat?'

The Inspector beside Posie crossed his arms tensely but, to his credit, didn't speak.

Posie swallowed the last custard cream hurriedly, tried not to choke on it.

'Quite the opposite, in fact,' said Posie hurriedly. 'I saw Norbert Carpenter earlier, in London. He asked me to come.'

She didn't add *to find out what happened.*

Because that would have been like a red rag to a bull for Inspector Vin. As far as he was concerned, he had already found out what had happened.

But at the mention of Norbert's name Posie observed a change in the girl.

Relief seemed to flood through Girvan, and a fire which hadn't been in her eyes before ignited and grew, and she stared at Posie intently.

'London?' she whispered.

Posie nodded.

'Then tell him I'm fine,' she whispered. 'I'm doing fine.'

'Who's this man you ladies are chattin' about?' asked the Inspector smoothly, sarcastically. 'Your fancy boy, is it, Mrs Briskow? The enigmatic priest? The solace of Sir Briskow's old age?'

Posie gripped the table hard. 'Is there anything you can tell me, Mrs Briskow, which would be useful for me in this case? To understand what happened better? Anything at all? Like *where* were you when the murder occurred? As far as I can tell you haven't given any details. Won't you tell me? Is there anything I can do to help? Norbert says you are not guilty of this crime.'

Girvan looked down at the table again. Her voice when it came was very small. 'There's no helping me now I fear.'

Inspector Vin suddenly seemed to lose patience.

'I think Miss Parker has had enough of this tripe for one evenin',' announced Vin suddenly.

He glanced over to his Duty Sergeant, and nodded. 'Lock 'er up again, will you? But don't yet throw away the key… They can do that in Norwich, where you'll be moved on Monday. It will be your last little trip, Madam. The point of no return, eh?'

And then he laughed uproariously. As if he'd made a good joke.

Posie frowned at Girvan as she was dragged to her feet, still silent.

Posie called out: 'I've read about your work, Mrs Briskow. It sounds an awfully good cause. When this is all over, I'll talk about making a donation to your project for girls, okay?'

But Girvan just stared at the floor as Inspector Vin made dismissive noises and made a show of clanging his metal chair feet across the floor.

Posie kept her voice carefully unexcited: 'Until tomorrow, then, Mrs Briskow. I'll sort this out.'

Rising, and chattering false-politely with the Inspector about little trivialities regarding the Norfolk weather, Posie tried to keep the man on side as they walked to the reception.

'Have there been any other developments in this case?' she asked sweetly. 'I used to know old Sir Briskow, you see. And Mrs Girvan Briskow, of sorts. This has all been a dreadful shock, I can tell you.'

Vin swaggered slightly, lit up another cigarette. 'I'll say, Mrs Lovelace. A shock for us all. And as to developments, well, somethin' nice and neat happened for us today. It was the readin' of the Will, see? Over at Marchpane & Marchpane's. And who do you fink gets *everythin'*?'

Posie couldn't guess. She hoped against hope it wasn't Norbert, because that would make things complicated.

Vin jumped in: 'It was your little Miss Friendly in there! Well, she don't get things outright. But the *whole lot* goes to this project you were talking about just now. A project for educating girls who are no better than prostitutes! Imagine. I say let them rot in hell, eh? But no: she gets the *lot*! It gives her the freedom to open more of these so-called 'colleges', and where she likes. God help us all! Before, it was only a sliver of the estate, a quarter, actually, but old "Boots" changed it the day before he died apparently. Sir Peregrine's own two remaining sons have been cut right out, and there's not even provision for the two crusty old servants who have looked after him for decades. A cryin' shame, I call it, and it gives the strongest possible motive for little Girvan, eh? Kill the old fella and get the money soonest, eh?'

Posie swallowed. She had to admit it didn't look very good.

'Did Girvan know the Will had been changed in favour of her 'colleges', sir?'

Vin looked nonplussed. 'Apparently they were *all* told by the old man that his Will was being changed, but he didn't disclose the full extent of the changes. Only told the solicitor, old Regulus Marchpane, when he entered the lawyer's office, and the old lawyer was pretty darn shocked, let me tell you.'

'Mnnn. Tricky motivation though, sir, unless you can prove beyond doubt that Girvan *knew* it was being changed. And anyhow, it's not for her. Perhaps she doesn't even know now?'

'Pah! Of course she knows. Her father-in-law must have told her. Or else she had sight of it somehow. *Why* Sir Peregrine would leave his money like that I have no idea, though. To dreadful low-life girls? What a mystery!'

Posie tamped down her anger and annoyance at the Inspector. 'Mnnn. So what happens to the Will now, sir? If Girvan is found guilty next week?'

'Hopefully the earlier Will comes back into play, Mrs Lovelace.'

Inspector Vin nodded approvingly. 'The older Will was split into four shares: one to each surviving son; one to Mrs Girvan; and one share to the servants, to be distributed equally. There *were* two other daughters-in-law, but both of them are now dead, and there is no survivin' issue. Mrs Girvan Briskow's share will fail, as she is the murderer, and her share will be added to the three shares which didn't fail. Pretty neat, hopefully.'

'Mnnn.'

The Inspector made a harrumphing noise which Posie took as dismissal. However, she wasn't done yet.

Now she put on her sweetest, most wheedling voice:

'Do you think, Inspector Vin, I could see the artefacts in this case? Photographs, if possible?'

Inspector Vin's snort of laughter turned into a retching cough, but he paled. 'You're really serious, Mrs Lovelace?'

'Deadly. And of course, I *will* tell my husband how helpful you were. He remembered you.'

She paused, and lied, only a little. 'He said you'd moved around the country to further your career. He said how well you ran things. Perhaps you could talk to him about a move to the city again? New Scotland Yard? I know he's recruiting inspectors just now.'

Vin puffed his chest up a little at this, but still looked caught off-guard.

'Well, all the evidence has been sealed up of course, ready to go to Norwich, with the prisoner in the police van. But I suppose there's no harm in you *looking* at it… No notes, mind. No copying of anything, Madam. I hope you understand?'

'Absolutely.'

'The photographs are not much fun for a lady, Mrs Lovelace: I must say. Pretty bloody. Are you sure you want to look?'

'Gracious, yes. Not much gets to me, you know. I used to work on the Western Front, you know. I saw worse out there than you can throw at me now, I'm certain of it. Sure as bread is bread.'

Besides which, I'm hearty, robust, and unafraid.

I could have done your job; in another lifetime, maybe.

She followed his reluctant figure back along the same white corridor, and stood behind him as he opened a cupboard much like a linen press.

A few bare shelves contained one or two shoeboxes. One was marked 'BRISKOW – NORWICH TRIAL' and he took it down and motioned for Posie to follow him.

Back they went to the interview room again, and Vin watched, smoking nervily, standing under a window, as Posie unpacked the box.

Brown envelopes, all marked 'EVIDENCE' contained the stash of Treasury notes, the gold fob watch, the black diamond brooch.

If these things could talk.

But they couldn't. Didn't tell her a wretched thing.

Then there was the packet of photographs, taken two weeks ago, at the murder scene. Posie steeled herself to go on, to really *look*.

She heard Vin cough in the corner, knew she only had seconds before he changed his mind and invented something which meant she could no longer look at these.

She scanned them urgently, willing herself to take everything in, and not to gag.

Here was the study, a place she had remembered well, as it turned out. Not much had changed.

Here was the framed photo of the woman in the corset, but now spattered in sticky blood, upturned next to two dark rings of residue on the desk-top. A pipe had been left uncleaned.

Here was the old man, smaller and much frailer than she could ever have thought possible. Hunched, lying dead, on one of those cosy rugs.

Here was blood, all over his front, a clear entry wound of a bullet in the chest of his white shirt, and here too was a close-up of his face.

A bullet had entered at the left-hand temple, and sticky tarry blood was pooled all over the carpet beneath.

The left temple.

Posie hurriedly moved through the other snaps.

The gun.

A Mauser. It had a long elegant barrel and a rounded grip shaped like a handle from a broom. Was it standard army issue? Posie pulled the picture right up to her face.

What a shame I can't take notes.

There was a serial number on the gun. But it was indistinct. 28-28-2004. Or was it 2007? The picture was blurry. Posie tried to memorise the number.

'Where is this gun itself now, sir? And how did Girvan Briskow come to have it, sir?'

Vin pursed his mouth. The question was unwelcome.

'The gun has been sent to Norwich already, Madam. It went with the body. And I cannot answer your second question. It was her late husband's revolver. Returned to her after the war, I suppose? Happened a lot.'

'I see. Thank you. Awfully good of you. I'll bid you goodnight then.'

And then Posie stepped into the cold, cold air outside.

She pulled her black wool coat collar up a little and clasped it for warmth as she walked in the gathering darkness.

Two shot wounds.

That had not been in the newspaper story, but it *had* been in the police case notes.

But there was something which troubled Posie about the police case notes, and its detail of the gun, the 'broom handle' Mauser, which she couldn't quite put her finger on.

It bugged and nagged at her.

The Market Square was emptying, with shops being closed up, and people shouting out late greetings and last-minute invitations to each other.

As Posie walked she thought of strange, proud Girvan.

Had Girvan known about the fortune awaiting her? To be administered by her to poor girls? At the cost of the loss of that fortune to others? *Had* she murdered the old man to get the money?

Ahead of her was Holly House, and it seemed that the lights twinkling out from the long elegant windows and the sense of movement within the place was more vivid than anything Posie had remembered from its past; from *her* past.

But she stopped dead in her tracks. She was standing right outside the lawyer's office, Marchpane & Marchpane.

With a slight shiver she imagined Harry standing with her; she remembered his pleasure in this place. That transitory, ephemeral gold plaque which had been his pride and joy.

Before she knew it, Posie was knocking at the door.

* * * *

Six

Regulus Marchpane was about two hundred years old.

Or at least he seemed it.

Posie stuck out her hand and introduced herself formally. But the old lawyer grinned toothily and waved her hand away.

'I remember you, Posie Parker. Henry Parker's daughter, and no mistake. A sad business, a sad business.'

'My father dying?'

'No, I meant your mother, Rosa. Damn fine woman. We heard about it up here, in the end. How she died. I'm not religious, and I never gave two hoots for your father, I'm afraid. He always struck me as an old-fashioned stick-in-the-mud.'

Posie laughed easily.

Mr Marchpane offered Posie a sherry, and she drank it in tiny sips, over the big green-tooled-leather partner's desk.

Regulus nodded thoughtfully. 'But there was your connection with Harry Briskow, too, of course. Linking you here…'

Regulus downed his own drink. Poured himself another.

'*Why* have you come back? Why are you here?'

'Er…'

'It's this Peregrine Briskow affair, eh? Well, that fits. I've read about you: you're a detective now? It's a good job you got away. In that, fate dealt you a lucky hand, eh?'

Posie gaped. 'Lucky I got away from here?'

'From it all. But as I said, you want to talk to me about Peregrine? I know it. Well, I can't say I'm surprised. That family were always going to pull themselves down in flames and now they have done just that.'

Posie half-grinned. 'Weren't your two families bitter enemies? So, you'd be bound to say something like that.'

'Not necessarily, my dear. The Marchpanes have always considered themselves as angels, fixing things. Sorting things out. Why, *you* know that, of course. I gave young Harry a partnership here, against the family odds.'

Posie countered back: 'But that was because you didn't have enough money to keep the business running alone. So you *were* sorting things out, practically, sir. But you weren't really being an angel, were you?'

'*Touché*, Miss Parker. *Touché*. And in the spirit of candour, Harry Briskow would not have been an ideal long-term partner.'

'Oh?'

'The family history, eating at us, Miss Parker. Tell me, what do you want to ask me about Sir Peregrine? The Will? How it is split?'

'No. I think I know all that. I wanted to ask you how he had been. Lately, I mean. I saw the police snaps at the police station, and he looked bad.'

'Death can do that to a fella, Miss Parker.'

Posie bit at her lip. 'Sick, I mean: shrivelled up. Not how he was when I knew him... Even with half his head blown away I thought he had an expression of relief on his face.'

The old lawyer sighed; all humour gone. 'You're right, Miss Parker. Of course you are. I shouldn't joke. "Boots" Briskow was a tortured man. He'd been my client for years, decades. The change I saw in him since his sons died was pitiful. In these last years especially he came to believe he was cursed; that the whole Briskow family were cursed. There *had* been odd goings on throughout the years; all that business with his wife, poor Emily, for example. And then other awkward moments when he must have wondered about a curse, for sure. But later, in 1917, with four boys dead... Well, it does things to the mind.'

'I'm surprised he lasted as long as he did, sir.'

'Yes, true. And then tragedy struck again last year, in June. Kate Briskow, Johnny's widow, died in that terrible coach crash near York, in Grassington, together with her two girls. They'd been here first, down from Scotland for their school holidays. They spent some days at Holly House, visiting Peregrine. Then they had a trip to Yorkshire planned on the way back. A dreadful affair. The only Briskow grandchildren, gone in a stroke!'

Posie shook her head in disbelief. It was all so, so sad.

She didn't blame Sir Peregrine for believing there was a curse on his family.

Although such things are usually a load of nonsense.

Regulus had filled his pipe and now he lit it, shaking the match out. He inhaled the sweet smoke and exhaled slowly.

When he spoke next, he sounded puzzled: 'Then, Peregrine had a sudden change in circumstances. He seemed to rally. Last autumn, Geoffrey, his soldier son, returned, and then so too did Girvan, Joseph's widow. I think Geoffrey had written to Girvan; asking her to visit. She was over in Belfast. She's only been here a few months, but I think she was a tonic. She gave Peregrine hope. Things to talk about. He was even seen in the town again. But then he had bad news only a month ago. The worst kind.'

'Oh?'

'He was told he was dying. Not much longer to go. Weeks, maybe? He came here, wanting to change his Will. He signed the new Will the day before he died. It's no secret. The family know now: I read it aloud to them all this morning. He had decided the Briskow curse would be vanquished. He decided to change his Will so that no male Briskow could benefit. *It was all to go to girls.* He was after penance, I think. Some kind of redemption. He certainly saw that snotty priest fella enough.'

Posie frowned. 'Norbert?' she asked, curiously. 'The Reverend Carpenter?'

'The one who sniffs and shivers all the time? Yes. They'd got quite close in recent months, although I rather got the impression that the Reverend came to Holly House *not* just for the sake of talking with old Peregrine, if you get my gist. There were other attractions there on offer.'

'Oh!' Posie frowned. 'Girvan?'

'Perhaps. You'll have to ask him, though, won't you?'

'Oh, I will.'

The old lawyer shook his head sadly. 'Well, it's a sorry old story, isn't it. Peregrine killed! And not for much reason that I can see. He was about to die anyway! Poor old fella. When I saw him the day before he died, he told me he'd seen a black dog in the house. It seemed to have spooked him horribly. What an end to a dreadful tale. The whole line blighted.'

Posie swallowed uneasily, then stood and buttoned up her coat.

She was running slightly late.

They walked to the big front door with its iron hinges and latches. A door Harry must have touched multiple times a day. This had been, after all, his whole world.

She liked this odd old man; she liked his bluntness. 'Do *you* believe Girvan Briskow did this, sir?'

He faced Posie squarely. 'Devils have had angels' faces before, Miss Parker. But you know that, of course.'

She was almost shocked at the impertinence of the statement. 'Gosh, do you mean my *mother*? I know she had a reputation for wildness but she was hardly a devil. Or did you mean my father? Because you're right: he wasn't a good man, I know that now. But he wasn't a devil either…'

The old man shrugged.

'I suppose I mean people we trust and hold dear. Friends, families, lovers. Those who have disappeared. In the end, we just have to hope they don't, or didn't, let us down. We can never really know. Goodnight.'

****

Posie stood outside Holly House.

She exhaled slowly. Had never thought she would be back here.

It was now completely dark and the lights sparkled inside brightly and cast long reflections out over the cobbled pavement in front of the house. Someone inside was playing the piano very loudly, and badly; it sounded like a jazz refrain. A shout went up.

Could it be? A party?

She clutched her carpet bag to herself and knocked at the lion's head doorknocker.

After a couple of minutes, a man opened the door, but it wasn't Wykham.

Posie got the shock of her life.

Silhouetted in the door was Harry.

Or rather, it was a man who resembled Harry. But older.

This is what Harry would have looked like if he'd lived…

Posie pulled off her hat, her gloves, stuck out her hand.

'I'm Posie. We spoke on the telephone. Mr Miles Briskow?'

Immediately she realised her mistake. This man, who suddenly grabbed at Posie in an enormous bearhug, must be Major Geoffrey Briskow, the professional soldier. Up close he had the weathered tanned face of a man who had spent decades out in a hot sun, his lilac eyes bright against his skin, his light brown hair almost flecked with gold.

He let Posie go and she almost tottered over.

This man was in his early forties, the current head of the family, and it was obvious he was blindingly, unnervingly drunk.

He stank of neat alcohol.

In his hand he held a glass with clear liquid in it, some kind of gin, or vodka perhaps? Around his neck was a red ribbon and it was full of keys. He raised his glass, clanking with the heavy keys like Marley's ghost.

'Posie? Posie, did you say? I don't care who the blazes you are but come inside. I'm Geoffrey and I'm toasting my dear dead daddy, and this is my final night *ever* on these wretched shores!'

He stepped inside.

Posie followed, and noticed the black and white tiled entrance hall was piled high at one side with battered leather trunks, luggage tags already affixed.

Next to the luggage was a set of golf clubs, fishing rods and a rifle. Geoffrey managed to follow Posie's gaze and he laughed gleefully.

'Yep, they're all mine. A one-way ticket to America. Tomorrow night. You want to join me, Polly? Dolly? What was it? *Rosie*? We can get married in the morning and make a dash for it, eh? I haven't a bean in the world but what do I care? I'm alive and I have my freedom! Come with me, Rosie?'

'Er, thank you, but no. And I'm Posie, by the way. Posie Parker.'

Another man was now in the corridor. Smaller, paler, bald, with the sad black eyes of the doctor brother, Joseph, who had died years before; too young, and for nothing.

This brother wasn't drunk, and he was wearing the long black gown of the professional prep school teacher.

He darted forward and smiled, hand outstretched. 'Forgive us, Miss Parker, we are at sixes and sevens here. My brother has decided to leave; and we've had some rather odd news today, on top of a lot of other jolly odd news lately.'

Posie thought she'd be blunt. 'The Will, you mean? With everything going to Girvan Briskow's destitute girls?'

Geoffrey laughed manically. 'You've heard? I expect the whole wretched world has heard about it by now. Well, *we've* done nothing to be ashamed of.'

And yet you're running away?

Miles ushered Posie into the green parlour. It was dimly lit and very cold. There was no fire on in the grate where a dead dog had once, or twice, been imagined.

'Do sit, Miss Parker. A drink?'

He went to a small glass trolley and started pouring brandy from a cut-glass decanter there.

Posie glanced around and remembered that first tea party years before; except now, of all the guests assembled there back then, she was the only constant. All the other guests at that party were dead, or *almost* dead, if you included Girvan's chances at her upcoming trial with Lord Justice Roade.

Rather than sit, Posie walked over to the window and glanced up to where the poor small angel was still painted on the ceiling, keeping the wolves at bay, holding a key aloft.

In the dim light she tried to take in the detail, and narrowed her eyes.

Could it be? Could it be that this angel was holding...

'Posie?' Geoffrey had strolled in languidly, and thrown himself down on a green velvet tasselled sofa, where he stretched out and yawned.

'Do join us.' He patted the seat beside him.

He played with the huge set of chunky keys at his breast. 'Who *are* you again?' he asked, in desperate confusion. 'I *do* know your name. You're some sort of police person?'

Posie thought back to that old advert from years before in the Reading Room at Holt Library and almost – very inappropriately – wanted to laugh.

But before she could answer, Miles butted in, passing over her drink.

'This is Posie Parker, Geoffrey. We never met her. She was Harry's fiancée.'

Geoffrey sat up immediately, ramrod straight. The humour dropped from his face like a curtain falling. 'Dear God! I'm so sorry. Sorry about you losing sweet young Harry like that…'

Posie shrugged. 'It should be *me* who is sorry. Let me offer my condolences on the death of your father. He was certainly a very original man.'

Geoffrey narrowed his eyes. 'I don't think you would have got to see the best side of him, somehow. Not if you were fiancée material.'

Miles cut in, shutting his brother up, polite yet firm: 'Did you have questions for us, Miss Parker, or was this a social call? Either are fine, but I wasn't sure when we spoke earlier, when you called from London.'

But before she could reply, old Wykham came in, bringing a silver platter of nuts, cheeses, pickles. As if they really *were* at a party.

Both Briskow men ignored Wykham as he set the food down on a low table, and then the Butler straightened up painfully.

Wykham must have been the same age as Sir Peregrine, and apart from the creaky back, he looked exactly as he had done last time Posie had seen him, during the time of the Great War. He was still very dignified, with a thatch of white hair and his crow-black, immaculate Butler's clothes.

He nodded very slightly over to Posie, and whispered an unobtrusive: 'Good evening, Madam'.

His eyes took in her black clothes and her sparkling

earrings, and her wedding ring, and he obviously approved.

He stood, arms behind his back, unobtrusively just outside the door.

Posie, for perhaps the first time since arriving, didn't know how to proceed. *Something was off.*

But what?

It felt as if an energy was trapped. She could almost feel the air humming between the repressed politeness of Miles and the extravagant drunk gaiety of Geoffrey with his desperate aim of running away.

She started with the Priest.

'Actually, I'm here because I was asked to meet the Reverend Norbert Carpenter. He was my father's old curate actually. I understood he lives here?'

Geoffrey hooted with laughter, amused. 'By Gad! The fella has strong nerves for a priest, eh? Well, "tell the truth and shame the devil": that's what our mother taught us, and that's exactly what he's done. Yes: he was here all the time, with Girvan, up in her rooms, although officially he had digs over at the King's Head, in Blakeney. An unusual sort of cove, Carpenter, isn't he? Our Pa turned a blind eye to their carry-on. He liked the priest, unusually. Must have listened to him, too: cutting us out of the Will and convincing him to leave it all to Girvan's waifs and strays.'

'Geoff!' barked Miles, suddenly in schoolteacher mode. 'We've already spoken about this. You and I were never reliant on Pa's money, and we have no need of it now. We have our own jobs!'

'Speak for yourself.'

'You'll get one, Geoff, in America. It's the land of opportunity, they say.'

It was Posie's turn to butt in. She spoke straight at Geoffrey, who, despite the alcohol, she found she could engage with better.

'I understood that the current Will may be overturned, Major? If Girvan is found guilty, your father's previous

Will would be reinstated, and then,' she looked about her, 'you would both be catered for.'

'Nonsense!' sneered Geoffrey. 'Why would she be found guilty? This is all a lot of tosh. A shindy over nothing. Little Girvan didn't kill our father: I'd trust her with my life, and I trusted her with my father's life, too. Pa always had a soft spot for her and I thought she would help him again now, which she *did*. She was a midwife and a nurse by training, not a killer. She pulled Pa out of the doldrums and turned his whole outlook around. Besides, she barely has the strength to pull the trigger on Joe's gun; it was a Mauser, which is what they say killed old Pa. She'd never be able to do it twice. Bally tough, unwieldy things, those 'broom handle' pistols. Have *you* ever tried shooting one, Miss Parker? And Girvan's a bally sight smaller than you!'

Posie shook her head. 'Can I ask you where the Mauser was kept, Major Briskow? Did Joseph's gun *belong* to Girvan? Did she keep it up in her room?'

But Miles cut in instead: 'The guns were kept by my father in his study, in a special gun cupboard there. When each of my brothers died, their effects were sent back here, eventually; to Holly House. Guns included.'

Geoffrey was swaying slightly, up on his feet. 'Would you like to see?' he asked eagerly.

Miles interrupted. 'Oh, it's rather morbid. I don't think...'

But Geoffrey jangled the set of keys at his neck. 'For one last night I am still the Head of the House, before fleeing the curse of the House of Briskow forever! You must all do as I say. If I say we will see the guns then we will see them! Let me give you a guided tour.'

He extended his arm to Posie, and she rose, a half-smile playing at her lips, keen to seem eager to join in, a party guest at the very oddest of balls.

Although, the reality was that Posie was caught off-guard.

She had never heard of effects being returned. Not once. If *anything* of Harry's had ever been posted back, surely she should have been allowed to keep something as a remembrance?

'In here! In here!'

Miles groaned in exasperation and trailed behind. They went along the corridor to the next room, and Wykham floated along silently ahead, flicking on the lights in the red study, then stood sentry-like outside.

Posie had seen this room in a black and white snap not an hour before, with Inspector Vin, and, because of those snaps, she found herself peering intently at the rug by the fire, where the body of Sir Peregrine had fallen, and at the desk where his spattered blood had landed.

The rug was now immaculate, the desk clean, the photo of Emily Briskow untainted. Sir Peregrine's pipe was back in position on his desk, wiped clean and looking as if it might be picked up at any moment.

The tobacco pouch next to it at the left-hand side was plump and ready.

Geoffrey was in the corner struggling with a massive, ugly portrait of a civil-war era woman with a hooked nose and a white cap. At last he threw it back on its hinges. Behind this was a metal cupboard built into the wall.

Geoffrey grabbed at the keys around his neck, squinted at them all, and started painstakingly trying to fit one after another into the lock. He made very slow and shaky progress.

'Oh, *here*. For goodness' sake.' Miles ripped the red cord from his brother's neck. 'It's a small bronze one. Flat head. *Here*.'

He rather ungraciously fitted the correct key in the lock and they all heard the 'CLICK' of metal in metal as the fastenings opened.

Miles pulled back the door.

Posie came right up behind the two brothers.

It took her a moment to understand what she was seeing.

A recess: green; felt-lined.

In it were four small bronze plaques, with each of the dead Briskow boys' names upon it, with their relevant dates. Medals were mounted beside three of the names; a variety of bright ribbons to indicate bravery, battles, or simply the lucky art of survival. Studio photographs, too. Of each son in his uniform.

But Harry's plaque had no medals, and no photograph.

Under each name, however, were two hooks, and on one was a man's cap, and on the other was a gun.

Posie's eyes moved quickly over this cabinet of sadness and horror, a horrible lump of numbness gathering inside.

She suddenly felt like crying; that burst of pepper-hot emotion that comes unannounced, spreading over your eyes and nose and flooding your heart with raw grief.

She gasped, tried to tamp the sadness down.

'Golly, I had no idea.'

Caps, in each case bloodied with black, ancient dried blood, were torn, crushed, pulled from the battlefield.

The guns were shiny, immaculate.

Her eyes registered Harry's cap. She remembered him wearing it, fresh and pressed neatly, at Sheringham train station. She had had no idea it had ever been rescued, or sent back. She certainly had never been informed. Why?

It was black with dirt and who knew what else, and there was a vicious-looking jagged rip through the top.

She went closer to touch it. She thought she had seen a glimmer of gold. Was she being fanciful?

But Miles exclaimed loudly. 'That's bally odd. Harry's gun is missing!'

Posie froze. Geoffrey frowned. 'Joe's gun, the Mauser, has been kept by the police, Miles. You know that. As evidence. They say Girvan hid it in her bathroom upstairs, although I'm sure it's all bally rot.'

Although you are running away, and not bothering to save her.

What she will face with Roade is no party.

Who will pull her out, if not me?

'No! Look again, Geoff,' insisted Miles. '*Harry's* gun is missing.'

And it was.

But there wasn't much to be done about it.

Both brothers said the gun cupboard had been their father's very private domain, and perhaps he had had reason to remove things? Or put them in different places?

As they argued Posie gently reached up and touched Harry's cap. She didn't try and pull it down; it was too high. But she moved it to one side.

Yes: she had been right.

Gold, a glimmer of gold.

There, under the cap, was a fine, fine gold chain, and on it was that tiny flat golden key which she remembered Harry wearing against his skin, hidden normally by his shirt. The key with the tiny carved angel wings.

Posie frowned. What was it doing there? Hidden by that old cap? Had it been sent back from the battlefield, taken from Harry's dead body?

She touched the tiny key for a second between thumb and forefinger; pinched it and tried to imagine a magic which wasn't there.

Why did he wear this? What was special about it? Even all these years later, she felt slightly curious.

She let the cap swing back into place quickly but in truth the brothers had hardly noticed what she was doing.

They were still bickering between themselves about Harry's gun. And Posie felt a nagging sense of worry.

She spun around the room, saw Wykham over by the civil war carved window seat. He was sitting down on it, and seemed weary suddenly. An old, old man.

His fingers gripped at the window seat and he looked strained.

Posie felt for him, too. If Girvan was found *not* guilty, Wykham would be cut out of a well-earned legacy.

Perhaps the Butler felt the heaviness of this truth now? She darted to him, over by the window.

'Wykham, can I ask you a question?'

'Of course, Madam. Anything.'

'Was Sir Peregrine in good spirits lately?'

'Oh yes, Miss. Very bright he was, which was a joy. After these last years of darkness. It was Mrs Girvan who did all that. She came back into his life and brought joy.'

'I see. And Sir Peregrine was in good health?'

'Never better, Miss. Quite a turnaround.'

'Thank you.'

Peregrine Briskow obviously hadn't shared his recent bad news about his health. Unless the lawyer, Marchpane, had got this all wrong?

Posie walked with the brothers back out into the hallway. Wykham followed closely. Her time was up, but everything felt more complicated than before, and worse, she felt unnerved.

The strange strands of this case wouldn't come together. Something was wrong at the core of this.

But what?

'Your father…' she said quietly, calmly to Miles. 'He was left-handed, wasn't he?'

Miles stared at her in puzzlement. 'I say, I really have no idea, Miss Parker. Is it important?'

'I doubt it.'

They had reached the front door.

'I say, if the Reverend Carpenter comes here, can you tell him I am staying at the Feathers Hotel? Across from here? He can contact me there.'

'Of course.' Miles nodded, polite rather than friendly. 'But I haven't seen him since Girvan was arrested. Actually, since before Pa died.'

'You're wrong!' slurred Geoffrey, leaning against the wall, now drinking from a hipflask.

'He was here last week, in Pa's study. We had a nice chat, although of course he was in a helluva state about Girvan. I think he was here for some of his things from upstairs. The study had been cleared and I was sitting there reading *The Norwich Mail*; I'd got to the page about Pa's murder, and about Girvan being tried. Carpenter kept pointing at the page, saying she hadn't done it. He asked me to clear her name. Said we needed to go for help… He asked me to come with him, but I confess I was a bit tied up right then.'

Miles puffed out his cheeks. 'You mean you were drinking, more like. Poor old Reverend Carpenter, he obviously gave up on you and went off for help elsewhere. Besides, you see *lots* of things Geoff, not many of them are real.'

He sighed, the practicalities of the tasks ahead of him almost weighing him down. Soon he would be the only Briskow left, the sole keeper of those heavy keys.

He looked worried: 'Now you mention it, Miss Parker, I'd better telephone to Blakeney, I suppose. Our father's funeral will be next week, *if* they release the body. I suppose Carpenter had better take the service; it would have pleased our father. He spent a lot of time with the Reverend here, in the study, in the end. The Reverend is very kind.'

Geoffrey laughed brashly. 'He is kind, and ridiculous! I'll be far, far away, but make sure you don't give out anything at the wake like we mixed up at Christmas, eh, Wykham?'

The Butler flushed slightly and his mouth took on a rueful line.

Miles scoffed, embarrassed. 'That wasn't anyone's fault, Geoff, least of all Wykham's. I don't even think poor Reverend Carpenter knew he was allergic to mulled wine like *you* made it… The house stank of it for two weeks afterwards. I personally never want to drink mulled wine ever again.'

Posie was intrigued.

Truth be told, she adored mulled wine, and said so.

Geoffrey Briskow immediately started listing out an exotic and complicated cocktail recipe which he'd picked up in India.

She lost track of the ingredients pretty quickly.

But it seemed that the main ingredient, a particularly potent nutmeg, which Geoffrey had brought back bags of from India, had caused the Reverend to spasm, and go into life-threatening shock.

Girvan Briskow's quick thinking and training as a nurse had resuscitated him, and then Norbert had spent a week in Holt Cottage Hospital, recovering.

Miles opened the front door now. He obviously wanted Posie gone.

'Good night, and good luck!' called out Geoffrey.

'Same to you,' said Posie softly.

And then she headed over to the bar of her hotel.

She had need of a telephone.

* * * *

Seven

Fox was still at work, as Posie had thought he'd be.

She asked for Lovelace but was told he was long gone. In fact, he'd left very early, hours before, in a pretty chipper mood.

Posie tried not to dwell on this and asked Fox to do two things for her.

'Could you check a gun registration number for me? It's a war revolver. And can you check a soldier's whole history for me, too? I'll be back here in two hours. I'm going for a fish supper. And I need to think.'

She *did* need to think.

But first she rang the pub in Blakeney, the King's Head, asking for Norbert Carpenter. If he was back from London it would be good to speak, and raise some of the anomalies which were worrying her in this case so far.

'Is the Reverend there, please? I understand he rents rooms?'

'That's right, luvvie. But he's not here right this minute.'

'Ah. Where is he? It's quite urgent.'

The pub landlady then came over quite conspiratorial, although she had no idea to whom she was speaking.

'Between you and me, I think Norbert may have done a midnight flit, dear. We have a spare chaplain here, young

Goodman, in another set of rooms, and he's been covering, on account of the Reverend Carpenter being so sick at Christmas. Goodman is here until Easter, so Norbert is freed of his duties, really. But Norbert told me two weeks ago he only wanted my rooms another three months because he was moving away. There's a *lady*, involved, if you get my drift.'

She coughed in a theatrical, nudge-nudge, wink-wink manner. 'Ever since before Christmas we've had funny goings-on upstairs; lots of *noises*. And he's been creeping about like a lovestruck schoolboy. Not that anyone would care! We'd all love to see him married. He *was* seen two Fridays ago, looking in the window of Clabe, the jewellery shop in Holt... The gold wedding ring section. Apparently he went inside. Imagine!'

'Gracious!'

Posie listened, rapt. It all sounded like things had been going quite apace for Girvan and Norbert, which was nice.

'When did you last see him, Mrs... er?'

'Sukey Brown, dear. I saw him two weeks ago *properly*, when we had that conversation about the rent of the rooms. But I heard him yesterday, upstairs. He was playing that horrible record of his, 'Hear My Prayer', is it? Over and over. A squeaky soprano boy singing; enough to shatter my nice clean windows, it is! And a load of horrible pounding organ music in the background. Enough to drive you mad! Sinister-sounding thing. Anyway, maybe he's gone away for a few days. Maybe to Norwich? You sound like you're not from here, by your accent? So you might not have heard about our big murder story... Well, it's quite possible his fancy lady is the *murderer*.'

Sukey Brown was breathless with excitement. 'Maybe he's gone to support her at her trial? Sorry, who did you say you were again?'

'I didn't.'

And Posie rang off, feeling more confused than before.

She walked around the War Memorial which she'd never seen before. It must have been erected only a couple of years before because the names on the marble were fresh and clear. It was well-lit, with two lamp posts on either side, and she saw that Harry's name was on it, together with his brothers.

She pulled away from the Memorial with a curiously empty feeling and floated down the High Street, the shops all now shuttered and dark. She bought fish and chips in the one open café, and took them in a greasy twist of newspaper and sat on a bench eating them carefully under a bright streetlamp.

She thought about Harry's dreadful wrecked cap from the Great War, and the necklace beneath it. She thought of his missing gun which hadn't been on the hook.

She thought of what the old lawyer, Marchpane, had told her about a curse on the House of Briskow, and how Peregrine Briskow had thought it could be put right. She thought of Peregrine's illness, and the change to his Will.

A bungled burglary, a shooting, and the arrest of Girvan, the girl who had brought happiness into the old man's life at the very end, but who also had, potentially, most to gain from the change to his Will. His seeing a black dog.

And then there was the question of the fleeing priest.

By Gad, but this was awkward.

However much she owed Norbert for looking after her father years before, you had to admit that things didn't look good for Norbert on current facts.

He and Girvan had obviously been in love, or lust, or something – here Posie squirmed – and had had a plan to get away, as proven by Norbert telling his landlady he was moving away, and the purchase of a wedding ring. That Norbert could be unconventional she had found out already, by his response to the young German couple in the Temple Church earlier today.

But where had they been planning on going? Back to Northern Ireland?

To start a new life there, running the projects Girvan had already set up for her destitute girls? Setting up more, in the same ilk?

And if that was the case, why wasn't Norbert implicated in this crime, too?

Surely the police would have investigated him? Why was all the evidence stacked up against Girvan and why was it just Girvan in that cold jail tonight?

If the couple had been up to no good, why would Norbert have encouraged Posie to help?

And why on earth, if Girvan wasn't guilty, did she not try to defend herself? Why didn't she say where she had been at the time of the murder?

Posie stood up, threw away the greasy paper and started to walk back.

She felt gloomy.

She must have walked this street with Harry hundreds of times. Forgettable times; *what on earth had they talked of?* She couldn't remember for the life of her. But they had sometimes held hands.

She'd always walked to the left of Harry, as he was left-handed, and she hadn't minded as this arrangement had usually kept her away from the filth of the road.

Left-handed.

Posie's thoughts were running nineteen-to-the-dozen. A kaleidoscope of shifting patterns moved for a second in her mind and made a proper but still very incomplete picture.

'Oh!'

Can it be?

She reached the corner of the Market Square, with Holly House up behind her, and was about to pause before crossing over to where the Feathers Hotel was, when she felt a sharp and staggeringly violent shove from behind, the force of which was enough to send her flying.

'Oh! *NO*!'

It was as if she was suspended in time, literally flying through the air, and then she was down on the hard, hard ground.

She scrabbled to get up, struggled on the slimy, slippy ground where her Mary-Jane shoes had no purchase at all.

A bus was just at that moment turning into the darkness of the Market Square, gathering speed, shifting gears and heading her way.

'Golly! No. Dear God, no!'

Posie tried to yell, but somehow the words didn't come.

Blinding lights were ahead of her. In front of her. All about her.

I didn't come back here to die like this, she thought, and she felt a terrible pain in her stomach, and that gut wrenching feeling of nausea again.

Lights out.

She closed her eyes, expecting it all to be over and she just prayed it was painless.

But suddenly there was a man in front of the lights, both his hands up, waving the bus down.

'WOAH! WOMAN IN THE ROAD. STOP! NOW! 'ERE! YOU'RE GOIN' TOO FAST, MATE!'

It was the lanky form of Inspector Vin, coatless, his breath steaming out in the cold night air.

'Get up, Mrs Lovelace, I'll help you. Come on!'

She felt hands tugging at her, under her arms, and then Vin, puffing slightly, indicated towards the bus with a flick of his thumb. 'I'll give that driver what for, don't worry about that: he was drivin' too fast. Although I dunno why you was in the road in the first place, Mrs Lovelace?'

And then, as Vin strode off, Posie saw Norbert Carpenter standing on the pavement, his moon-face sheeny in the darkness.

Posie dusted herself down. 'Gracious, I'm pleased to see you, Reverend! I thought you'd done a runner, actually. I couldn't think what had happened to you, other than that you had stayed in London, especially as you'd told your landlady that you're leaving.'

Norbert laughed wearily. 'I wasn't going far! I've been offered *here*, the town of Holt, as my main parish, and I've accepted. It comes with a big Vicarage, and Girvan and I have decided to wed. I'd proposed, as you may have found out, but officially it's still a secret. We were actually going to tell Sir Peregrine on the day he died. Start life together, here. Girvan wanted to be near to old Peregrine. Until the very end. He was very sick. She wanted to help nurse him.'

'You weren't going to Belfast? To run Girvan's colleges? I understood Sir Peregrine was going to leave her money for them?'

'Yes: wasn't it wonderful? Not restricted to Belfast, though. Peregrine and Girvan discussed setting up a college in Norwich. There are poor destitute girls even here; workhouse children who end up as working girls, who in turn are easy prey for violent men and dangerous criminals.'

Posie nodded. 'I'm surprised Sir Peregrine was interested, though.'

'Perhaps he thought Girvan could make a good go of it? What with her background in nursing, and women's voting rights, and also the whole midwifery side. She wanted to train these girls up for a vocation, but help them if they were in trouble, too.'

'Well, maybe Girvan still *can* make a go of it? I think I know what happened here now. I'm going to organise a meeting at Holly House tomorrow. You'll come?'

Norbert smiled and relief flooded his face. 'Thank the Good Lord. Of course I'll come: I wouldn't miss it for the world. What time?'

But then Posie heard her voice being called from behind.

Turning, she saw a small crowd of people were getting off the bus which had nearly just killed her. It had pulled up on the other side of the square.

Was that *really* Richard there? Silhouetted against the bright lights and with a suitcase on the ground? She'd recognise his stocky, reliable bulk anywhere. He seemed to be talking to two uniformed bobbies, in some detail; one of whom was taking careful notes. *What was he up to?*

Norbert Carpenter crinkled his weak eyes against the bus lamps. 'Oh, is this your husband, Posie?'

'Yes. Thank Goodness. He'll help us.'

'He looks most reassuring.'

She wanted to run to Lovelace, to feel his strong arms all around her, wanted to feel him pick her off the ground and tell her everything would be fine; she wanted to breathe in his fresh Blenheim-bouquet scented body.

But more than that she wanted to say: *Someone just tried to kill me.*

And I think I know who.

Turning to say goodbye to Norbert, she saw he had already gone, but Inspector Vin was back again, telling her how the bus driver had been well and truly admonished.

'Thank you *so* much for stopping that bus, Inspector. Now, could you do something else for me, Inspector?'

'Er… well, Mrs Lovelace. I was just getting on home to my digs. It *is* Friday night, but go on: what is it?'

'My husband has just arrived, so he can help you, if you like? Can you organise me a meeting at Holly House tomorrow morning? Say, ten o'clock? Please can you make sure the solicitor, Mr Marchpane, is there. And the Briskow brothers. All the household servants, too. And you'd better put an "all-ports" warning out, in case one of them tries to escape. I know Geoffrey already has plans for America. He needs to be stopped, immediately.'

Vin gulped, but then nodded, so Posie carried on. 'And please make sure Girvan Briskow is there, too, and in something nice and warm to wear, not that old striped bag. No handcuffs. Oh, here. I almost forgot!'

She took off her gloves and quickly snapped off her diamond and sapphire earrings.

'Here. I'd like you to give these to Mrs Briskow please. Please can you tell her they are always very lucky earrings? And that I think she deserves to wear them. Oh, and I need one last thing: there were *two* bullet wounds on Sir Peregrine's body, but I can't recall seeing the forensic testing reports on two bullets. Only one. Could you check the forensics report, Inspector? I haven't actually seen it.'

Inspector Vin shook his head, cautiously putting the earrings into his inner suit jacket pocket.

'We haven't got it, Mrs Lovelace. I haven't seen it either. The Pathologist was at Norwich Hospital, which was where the body was taken. He telephoned me and read the forensics report down the telephone to me, and I just took notes myself. I added my notes to the official police case notes.'

He added, slightly quieter: 'I didn't actually ask for the forensics report to be sent on. Didn't think it was necessary. Thought it was an open-and-shut case.'

Fool.

Posie tried not to make it look like she was judging him; she needed him on side.

'And do your recall if the Norwich Pathologist read out the details for one bullet, or for two?'

There was a slight pause. 'Er, I can't recall exactly, Mrs Lovelace. I think one; a match for that Mauser belonging to the prisoner's dead husband.'

'I see. Well, it's just possible something may have been missed. You need to get hold of that forensics report, or have it read out to you all over again. And can you check the general health of the deceased? If it's not in the Pathologist's report then you might speak to Sir Peregrine's local doctor. Get a sworn statement.'

'Where do you think we are, Mrs Lovelace? Things move slowly here. It sure isn't London.'

'No,' murmured Posie regretfully. 'It's not, is it?'

She was missing it already.

* * * *

She'd picked up Fox's messages, and stood at the window of the hotel bedroom with her hand on her stomach, holding the place where it had hurt in the fall. She was thinking about Fox's answers, weighing up their significance while Richard had a bath along the corridor.

A fire crackled cosily in the grate.

Her face was bruised and her eyebrow cut, but otherwise she was fine.

Richard was worried by the report of Posie being pushed into the road, and had sworn they were leaving Holt the very next day.

He came to her now and put his wet dripping arms around her from behind, and they both looked out across the dark square.

You could just see Holly House from here, and the offices of Marchpane & Marchpane, too.

Richard was kissing her ears, pressing up against her.

'Wait a minute…'

Posie closed her eyes. She needed to explain.

'I had a man,' she said, simply. 'Here, in Norfolk. Here in Holt. It was another lifetime ago. We were engaged. I was very young. I thought he was an escape. A springboard to a life I didn't have. I've never spoken about him to you because he meant shamefully little to me, really… but there were secrets in his family. Big secrets. They're all coming out now. And I'm beginning to think I wasn't as clever as I thought I was at the time: I *still* don't understand those secrets, even now.'

Richard smiled, his red hair dark with water.

'We all have secrets, darling girl,' he muttered, kissing the top of Posie's head. 'I've had other women too. I was married before, for goodness' sake!'

Posie tried not to think of the recent whiffs of amber perfume, the doubts she had had about him lately.

Perhaps she had imagined it all; he *was* here, wasn't he?

He sighed, a little sadly. 'Perhaps it's time to let go of the secrets which are troubling you so much? Dash it all, I don't care about who was in your life before, as long as you're in mine now. This is *now*, darling. All we have is now. By some crazy awful coincidence, I'd actually booked you a weekend up here; that nice Blakeney Hotel? It was Rufus who gave me the idea actually: said how lovely it is here; how much you'd enjoy a break. I'd planned that we would travel up here together. And then when you said you were coming here this afternoon I thought heck, I'll just follow on and we can try and take our chances wherever we find them. Look here…'

He went over to his coat, fumbled in the top inside pocket. He pulled out a dark green box from the Burlington Arcade. 'I picked it up this morning.'

He passed it across.

Posie opened it. A plain rose-gold ring was inside. On the front, in the middle, was an entwined 'RR' symbol; two initials around a tiny ruby heart. Then, curling outwards were more initials: a 'P', and a 'K' and another 'K'. *Phyllis, Katie, Kit.*

'That's all of us,' smiled Lovelace. 'Our family: no more and no less. Just perfect, just how we are. We don't need any more children, or anyone else. We're just fine.'

Posie slipped the ring onto her right-hand ring finger. It wasn't what she would have chosen in a hundred thousand years and yet it was utterly beautiful, and suited her entirely.

'It's perfect,' she grinned.

'Happy early Valentine's Day, darling.'

His voice was low, soothing. 'Tomorrow we'll leave here after this meeting you've called. You can show me the bit of seaside you always talk about, and we'll stay, if you fancy it. I've got one of Vin's constables to organise us a hired car, that's what I was asking him to do tonight, and we can always drive on somewhere else. On down the coast, or into Suffolk? Anywhere you like, eh? I'm on holiday. And so should you be.'

He pulled her even closer, if that was possible.

'By Gad, I can't wait any longer, my darling. Now, bally well come here…'

* * * *

Eight

The next day Posie dressed in her silver clothes again, not black.

After a good breakfast she walked arm-in-arm with Richard over to Holly House, where there were two constables on either side of the front door.

Rather over-egging the pudding, she thought. But then Vin had much to play for here.

And he'd played ball so far: organising the doctor's report, checking the forensics report at Norwich, staying up more than half the night making calls.

Vin nodded importantly at Lovelace, who was wearing off-duty flannels, in relaxed mode.

Wykham had done a sterling job of putting chairs around in a circle in the red study, and the two Briskow brothers – Miles, suspicious and irritable, wearing his schoolmaster's gown, even on a Saturday, and Geoffrey, puffy and subdued – sat nearest the cleaned hearthrug, while Girvan Briskow sat near the desk.

The fire was unlit and the room was deathly cold. You could see your breath. There was no tea, no coffee, no cakes.

Wykham stood sentry by the door, as was his usual stance, and then an older woman, the Housekeeper, Mrs Noakes, Posie presumed, came and stood next to him, prim, dour, with frazzled grey hair, in a black dress.

These two were brother and sister, Posie remembered, and yet there was something else about Mrs Noakes which was slightly familiar, but Posie couldn't think what exactly.

Then old Regulus Marchpane appeared in off-duty tweeds and joined them, bundled up in a thick coat, taking a seat in the circle, too. He played with his old battered green hat, flipping it up and down in his lap, probably to keep his hands warm.

Girvan's eyes went ceaselessly over to the door, waiting, expecting.

She was dressed in a plain navy woollen dress, and Inspector Vin had been as good as his word; Girvan looked neat and clean. She even wore a dash of pale pink lipstick. She also wore Posie's Cartier earrings and Posie was glad: she normally didn't believe in lucky talismans but these had never failed her yet.

Lovelace flung himself atop the window seat, leaning backwards against the wall, hands locked behind his head, casual as you like, injecting an informality to the proceedings which was welcome. He lit up a Turkish and blew out his smoke with enjoyment, offering one to Vin who took it with a nod of thanks.

Posie stood up, taking charge.

She had butterflies in her belly, and they mulched together, thrashingly real. She too had hope that Norbert Carpenter would arrive, although in fairness he hadn't known the exact time of the meeting. But hopefully he would slip in soon.

She twisted her new and unexpected Valentine's ring on her finger and found that it gave her a good deal of courage.

'Welcome everyone,' she said, meeting everyone's gaze, one by one. 'We are here because a grave wrong has been committed.'

'A "wrong"? You could call our father's murder that, yes!' muttered Miles, irritably. He was checking his watch, nervy. His manner today was unfriendly, uncooperative.

Posie bit at her lip and drew blood. 'Whatever the case, Girvan Briskow is *not* the person responsible for your father's death.'

'I knew it! I knew it!' muttered Geoffrey. Girvan's face was blank, unreadable; her eyes were still on the door.

Posie picked up the local doctor's report which Vin had handed her that morning. Vin's notes about the two bullets were scrawled along the bottom of it in bold capitals.

She carried on: 'What is interesting in this case is that we have a death which *looks* like a murder, only it is not. What we have is perhaps worse. Something *dressed up* as a murder, plus a whole lot of other danger and dreadfulness piled on top.'

Inspector Vin coughed politely. 'How is a murder not a murder, Mrs Lovelace?'

'When it is a suicide,' said Posie simply.

'WHAT?' yelled Miles. 'NO! You're wrong!'

Posie shrugged. She waved the doctor's report in the air.

'*Why* am I wrong? Your father had just been diagnosed with a serious, terminal, painful illness, and he knew he had only weeks to live: cancer in its rarest, most advanced form. He kept the diagnosis secret from the family, but he decided to change his Will; to change everyone's destiny. Then he was done. Finished. He'd had enough. He shot himself with one of the pistols he kept in here. The shot wound was in the left temple, simply because he was left-handed. I'd noticed this left-handedness before, when I came here years ago. The way he did everything with his left hand; especially the way he smoked his pipe.'

'I don't know about him being left-handed.' Geoffrey had folded his arms and he seemed intrigued. 'I was away for most of my adult life; I don't recall. But in the months since I returned, I *do* know that Pa was always alone here on a Friday afternoon, which is when this happened. So if he planned to kill himself, then that would have been the ideal time.'

Posie nodded. 'I propose to you all that Peregrine Briskow lay on that rug, dead, with his head half shot off, by his own hand. But then he was discovered.'

Lovelace had read Posie's notes over breakfast. He pointed at the Butler. 'It was you, man, Wykham, who called the police, wasn't it?'

Wykham stood up tall. 'I did call the police, sir. Yes. I discovered the body upon my return from the bank. But it was definitely a burglary, Madam. Hell of a mess in here.'

Posie shook her head.

'With respect, Wykham, I believe you are wrong about the burglary. And I believe,' she looked over at her husband, 'that Wykham was *not* the first person who discovered the body. Some things were unusual that Friday. And Sir Peregrine had not been quite alone in this 'empty' house at two o'clock. Although he had *imagined* he was alone.'

Posie turned to Girvan. 'Won't you talk now, and save yourself, Mrs Briskow?'

But the woman stayed silent.

Posie sighed. 'It was two o'clock. And, while the house is normally empty, on this day, up on the third floor, Girvan had her lover in bed with her. He had just proposed marriage to her.'

Posie watched the girl's face colour dark beetroot, but there could be no going back now. No way of explaining things without this part of the story.

'Girvan and her lover heard a strange noise; a shot rang out. Girvan sent her lover down to see what was happening, and Norbert Carpenter, for it was him, came in here. *He* discovered the body.'

There were several gasps, and both Briskow sons shot horrified looks at their sister-in-law, but she just stared down at the floor.

Posie faltered very slightly. 'I'm not sure exactly what happened next, but I suppose Norbert would have said a prayer. Sat on the hearth rug there? Possibly he picked up the gun which was in the old man's hand? That gun was Harry Briskow's, by the way, the significance of which I am still unsure of. But the forensics report confirms the bullet in the temple is compatible with the 455 Webley revolver; and *that* was certainly Harry's gun. I have heard from London with the confirmation, and with the serial number. It was also the only Webley here; the other brothers all had different makes.'

'Where does this take us, Posie?' asked Lovelace. The relaxed pose was gone. He was on the edge of the window seat. 'At this point it's still a simple suicide?'

'Yes. But then someone else arrived home and entered Sir Peregrine's study. Remember, Girvan upstairs had no idea what was happening at this point. She decided to wait it out upstairs.'

Still Girvan sat silently.

'A soldier came home, saw what had happened. I believe he and Carpenter must have spoken, both very shocked, and the soldier left the study, much shaken, and went to get drinks. Strong, strong alcohol. Returning to the study with the drinks the two men might have toasted the life of Sir Peregrine? They drank quickly, both of them very shocked and upset. I saw the rings of the residue of those two drinks in the photographs of the crime scene. But then things happened quickly.'

Everyone in the room was staring at Posie intently, gripped.

'Our second man went to the still-open gun cupboard, and he took out another gun. It was Joseph's gun, a Mauser. With the training and skill of his years of army life he shot at the body, through the heart. This was our second bullet, from the Mauser, but it wasn't the one which killed the old man. You heard it, upstairs, didn't you, Girvan?'

The woman looked up.

She nodded. Spoke at last. 'I had no idea what was happening. I didn't know if there were intruders. So I stayed hidden.'

Vin had gone to stand beside Geoffrey Briskow. He was fidgeting with a pair of handcuffs.

Lovelace was confused. 'But *why*, Posie? What's the motivation? The reason for the second bullet?'

'That's what the Reverend Carpenter couldn't understand. They'd drunk together and then this performance with the second gun had occurred, and perhaps Carpenter was watching the soldier, who he knew well and liked, starting to do something which was inexplicable: deliberately going around the study causing havoc; pulling out drawers and pocketing a watch, a brooch. I suppose he would have protested, but it would all have been fruitless.'

Lovelace was standing. Authoritative.

Yes.

He nodded over at Vin, who opened the handcuffs quickly, then snapped them onto Geoffrey's wrists.

Geoffrey Briskow looked as if he might be sick, but didn't protest once.

Posie was still astounded at the malice, but also the pride in the plan which she now outlined.

'While he had been making drinks, this whole idea with the second bullet came to our soldier's mind. It was a plan which was easy in the execution, and solved two problems. Two birds, one stone. The first problem was that suicide is never nice, and our soldier wanted to protect Sir Peregrine's reputation. Our soldier is proud, but he liked Sir Peregrine a great deal, too. Better by far to make it resemble a murder, or manslaughter.'

Posie looked at Geoffrey quizzically, noting his pallor beneath the suntan.

'The second problem which could be solved through all of this pantomime was much more satisfying. It was, of course, to do with money. But the repercussions were deadlier.'

Miles called out. 'Money? You mean Geoffrey wanted to frame Girvan for the murder? So the new Will would be overturned?'

Posie nodded. 'Precisely. A murderer or a murderess cannot benefit from their crimes under English law.'

Geoffrey shouted out desperately, rallying, pleading: 'But I had no idea until yesterday that the Will had been changed! Had no idea we had been excluded. Why would I do this? I was out, anyhow. At the links! Playing golf. You can check.'

Posie was almost done. 'The body of Sir Peregrine now had a peculiar shot at the left-hand temple, and a shot in the chest, but our soldier hoped that the fact Harry's gun was used first would go unnoticed, and so it did, until now.'

Inspector Vin had the good grace to blush, but he pulled at Geoffrey harshly, blustering.

Posie shrugged. 'In order to frame Girvan, our soldier simply needed to remove some items of value, then hide the 'stolen' effects, including her dead husband's gun, the Mauser, in such a way that would implicate her without any room for doubt. I think too that there must be a deeply personal aspect to this story: one I do not know about. I can only assume that Girvan Briskow had caused hurt or pain to the soldier at some point, and this hurt was deep and needed to be assuaged. Whatever the motivation, he hoped that the old Will would be brought back into place.'

Posie turned, whip-sharp on the solicitor. 'Isn't that how it works, Mr Marchpane?'

Suddenly the old solicitor, Marchpane, stood up. There was no more hat twirling.

'That is quite correct, Madam.' He seemed to want to say more. But he halted.

Posie had pulled out Fox's note from last night in front of her. She had asked him to find out all about a particular soldier, and he had done so.

'Of course, when I talk of a soldier, I'm talking not of one from the Great War, but rather a soldier from the Boer War. Fearless in battle and honourable off duty. A man whose family had once been very grand, but only on his mother's side, and even on that side they had got poorer and poorer.'

Everyone stared over at Marchpane, still on his feet, but Posie shook her head.

'It was you, Wykham,' Posie explained softly, turning directly to the Butler. 'The soldier I asked for information about was *you*. You served Sir Peregrine well after your years as a soldier, even though you should have been enemies, because by birth you were a Marchpane.'

Every eye was on Wykham, who stared back resolutely at the red wall where the long windows were, where Lovelace was still standing, arms crossed, bulky.

The old solicitor, Regulus Marchpane, sighed and shook his head sadly.

'I am much afraid *I* have things to answer for here. When I listened to your summary, Madam, just now, I thought I recognised the honourable intentions of a Marchpane at work. I have told some of you before that the Marchpanes all regard themselves as being on the side of the angels, fixing things. These actions here have all those characteristics, but they are obviously warped. Jeremy Wykham, my cousin, was always a clever, headstrong lad. As is his sister, Nora Noakes.'

Everyone looked over at the Housekeeper, insignificant as dust, but she kept her head up straight.

Posie sighed. 'I suppose you all meet up sometimes, you three cousins?'

The solicitor nodded reluctantly.

She pressed on: 'And I suppose you talk. Perhaps you talked to your cousin Jeremy about the Will of Sir Peregrine which had been changed two weeks ago, very much out of his and his sister's favour?'

Marchpane swallowed. 'It may have come out, yes. But they were both resolute. Disappointed, yes. But they promised not to say anything. Jeremy certainly didn't give me the impression he was about to start some campaign of madness in order to re-retrieve that share, the very next day…'

The Butler moved towards his sister, held her hand tightly.

Posie spoke directly to the pair. 'I think you *weren't* resolute about the Will; you were both devastated. You did what a good soldier does, Mr Wykham: you were opportunistic and you took a chance when you saw it. You knew you could incriminate Girvan, and so you did. But what on earth had she done to *you*? Why did you hate her so much?'

Suddenly Mrs Noakes, the Housekeeper, threw back her head and laughed hysterically. When she whipped her head up again, she fixed Posie with a dreadful stare, her lips curled back, her eyes wild.

'Hate?' Mrs Noakes hissed, and Posie realised it was the first time she had ever heard the woman speak.

'What do *you* know of hate? Coming here from London with your fancy ways and your fancy clothes and your big important fella. My daughter Millie was a good girl, just the same age as you. Oh, yes: I remember you, Miss Parker, even if you don't remember me. *Or* my Millie.'

'Millie?' Posie remembered suddenly the housemaid she'd met once here. Puffy-eyed and teary and dour, and she suddenly saw the resemblance between Mrs Noakes and that girl from so many years ago.

'I didn't know she was your daughter, Mrs Noakes. But of course, I do remember her. The charming red hair?'

Mrs Noakes nodded slightly. 'She *was* my daughter: yes. And she got herself into trouble, if you know what I mean. And then your Mrs Girvan here and her doctor husband, Joseph, with their 'caring' ways and 'modern methods' had her taken away and 'sorted out'. There was no baby to miss, to grieve for. And when she came home from that operation my Millie was never the same again. But Mrs Girvan here, she couldn't stop sticking her nose in, could she? She seemed desperate to get Millie away from me, from this house. Next thing we know she's enrolled her at a Labour Agency and Millie was doing all sorts of jobs not fit for a woman. From 1914 onwards Millie was working in a nasty filling factory and then she started to turn bright yellow, and started spitting up blood and all her teeth. Millie got so sick she barely knew who she was no more, but it took her six months to die like that; in utter agony.'

Mrs Noakes let out a strangled sob. 'So, Miss Parker, you ask about hate? I'll happily share some of mine with you, shall I?'

Girvan had turned around fully now, and she frowned at Mrs Noakes. 'I'm so very sorry for your loss. About Millie and that job: I *really* had no idea about the toxicity involved in those munitions' tasks, believe me. I *had* told Millie to stick to the trades: the post office and the dairy and the bakers, but she said she was after better pay. And those factories paid crazy money. Now we all know why. So sad.'

'Pah!' muttered Mrs Noakes, dabbing at her eyes with her apron, but she slunk down on a chair and put her head in her hands, defeated in life yet again.

Vin was confused. He had dropped his iron grip on Geoffrey, but the handcuffs were still in place. Brow furrowed, he turned to Lovelace.

'But, sir, has there even been a crime? I mean, Sir Peregrine was already dead, wasn't he?'

'Crime, Inspector?' Lovelace raised an eyebrow. 'Police obstruction, for a start, and falsifying evidence for a second. Letting a woman be tried for a murder she didn't commit must carry some penalty at law, too.'

Lovelace turned to Girvan. 'Can't you speak, Mrs Briskow? Help us out. Why didn't you say any of this when you were arrested?'

Girvan Briskow's eyes flashed fire.

She stood, facing up to Lovelace.

'Have you any idea what it was like here?' she said in her strong, clear tones.

'Madness. Lots of police, led by this *one*,' she indicated to Vin with a hand, 'going through everything. My underclothes, *everything*. The man whose house I lived in was dead, and the man I had just become engaged to had suddenly disappeared. I had no idea what was happening. I started to think that perhaps there had been an altercation? That perhaps Norbert had shot the burglar and run away in fear? I wondered too if poor Norbert had accidentally shot my father-in-law. All I knew, when he didn't return, was that he was gone, and so I sat here waiting. It was uncharacteristic of Norbert. I was waiting for a sign, which didn't come. It became clear to me over the next couple of days that I had been set-up. They said I'd killed Peregrine, had all the evidence of it, it was incontrovertible... I prayed, and I waited. God had shown me mercy before, giving me a good husband. He had almost given me another, and now I had to wait for his help. But God works in strange ways, and he sent me Posie Parker instead. A girl I hoped not to see again here.'

Lovelace flicked his head in Wykham's direction.

'You can arrest him, Vin. Get Mr Geoffrey Briskow released and then use the same cuffs. But we need to get the missing information. We look like fools. And most of this investigation has been shoddy, half-hearted. Where the blazes is Harry Briskow's Webley now? And where on earth is the Reverend Carpenter? If Mrs Briskow here is telling us the truth, which I believe she is, then her fiancé is a key witness. Why on earth didn't he raise the roof when he saw what Wykham was up to, setting up a fake burglary? I would have bellowed the place down, and protested like billy-o.'

Wykham was a big man, Posie saw that now, as the slighter Inspector Vin squared up to him.

She wondered if, for a second, Wykham might break into a run.

However, although he was big and still strong, he was old, not fast. The constables at the door, sensibly placed, she had to admit, would be a match for him and would bring him down.

Resistance was futile, but Wykham's cooperation was not a given.

She turned to the man, met his steely blue gaze, a gaze which had seen much and hoped for more.

'Did the Reverend Carpenter come here this morning? Have you restrained him, or hurt him? Worse? Please tell me where he is, sir.'

'I am afraid I really couldn't say, Miss Parker.'

It was ridiculous.

She'd seen Norbert Carpenter in London the day before, and then again last night on the Market Square.

He'd been heard in his rooms playing music two days before. Geoffrey Briskow had seen him a week ago, here, when he had asked Geoffrey to help, to intervene for Girvan.

So why was a rising sense of panic enveloping her?

A dreadful cold feeling of unease like a fog settling all about her?

Why had he been asking others to help, as if he couldn't himself?

She thought suddenly of Norbert speaking to her in the church, and his reverence for the choirmaster, Mr Thalben-Ball, who hadn't replied to him.

A horrible thought came to her.

But that wasn't possible.

Was it?

And then Posie fought off a sudden sharp wall of nausea which threatened to overwhelm her.

'Oh, dear God.'

Posie crouched to the floor, pain pulsing through her stomach.

'Posie? By Gad, darling, what is it?'

Lovelace was down on the floor with her, desperate. She felt as if she had been thrown in front of the bus again.

Looking up, she saw Wykham, now in handcuffs, staring at her, a slight mocking light in his eyes.

'It *was* you, sir, wasn't it? You followed me last night. You pushed me into the path of that oncoming bus? I was getting too close. I'd remembered that Sir Peregrine was left-handed, and had started to think about his death as a suicide. But was there something else I'd got too close to?'

Girvan Briskow was down on the floor with Posie too. 'Can I help? I am a nurse, years ago, but the training, it doesn't really go away. I wonder, are you…? Oh, by the Grace of God, what's that dreadful stink?'

Cinnamon. Spices. Nutmeg.

Posie shook her head. 'I can't actually smell it, but I think it's because it's always with me now. I'm impervious to it.'

She struggled up, and Lovelace held her tightly.

'You need to clear this room of everybody,' Posie whispered to him. 'Everyone needs to go, except the solicitor.'

'Even Wykham?'

'Yes. He won't say a thing more. And you'd better bring those constables back, with axes, saws, screwdrivers.'

****

Nine

So much in life was broken, thought Posie to herself. So much was inexplicable.

She'd had cases before where whole sections of them couldn't be explained properly. Not rationally.

But here, the one thing which had been constant had been Norbert Carpenter, and his hope that Posie could fix things.

Like he had once fixed things for her, and her family.

Posie stood silently at the window nearest the door, watching.

She was staking a lot on a hunch here, and it was a rather wild one. She'd get the local police force, and Lovelace himself, in big trouble if she was wrong. The damage would be irreparable.

But it was important.

Lovelace was looking at Posie with the slightly twisted-about-the-mouth expression he always wore when he wasn't quite certain of things.

Posie watched as old Regulus Marchpane drew a map. It was fairly basic, rudimentary. A twist here, a turn there, a door here.

'My great-grandmother taught us. Me and my cousins, Jeremy Wykham and Nora Wykham, as children. My great-grandmother was the last Marchpane to know the secrets of these tunnels. This was her house, and she knew it well. But I say! My memory is not what it was.'

Lovelace was struggling with the window seat. 'How do you open this thing though?'

Marchpane shrugged. 'Actually, I must confess I don't know how, anymore. There were once keys, but they are all long gone. My great-grandmother had the last of them. Beautiful little thing with carved wings upon it. She showed us how it worked, and she wore it like a charm. It was the only one that remained. She said she was the custodian of it: every generation had its own angel who would look after it. I think it got lost when she died.'

He finished his map, thrust it at Lovelace.

'The main entrance at the heart of the complex is in the green parlour; below the painted angel. The little fella holding the protestant wolves of Norfolk at bay? That particular entrance is very clever and it contains a 'safe room' built right under the green parlour, which then leads out into the whole warren of tunnels. But all the window seats here are interconnected. They act as direct entrances into the tunnels below. The one in *this* study will go straight down to the tunnels. You have to climb down. There are clever inbuilt steps. It's a long drop.'

Lovelace sighed. 'Right, lads, we'll just have to force the thing open.'

Posie was thinking nineteen to the dozen, and what Mr Marchpane had just said was re-playing in her mind: a key, with angel wings; a charm.

Angels.

Every generation had its own angel.

She remembered Harry's reluctance to explain his necklace to her, all those years ago, before he left for war.

I'll tell you about this another time.

Posie shook her head. 'I don't think that key got lost, Mr Marchpane.'

Posie rushed to the ugly painting of the lady in the corner. 'It's in here. There's a gun cupboard behind here, and that angel-wing key is in here, I swear it. Geoffrey had the key to this gun cupboard, on a big red cord. But Geoffrey and Miles don't know what the angel key is for, but Wykham *did* know, of course. It would have been easy enough for him to access this gun cupboard after Sir Peregrine's death.'

Marchpane looked genuinely surprised. 'Jeremy Wykham? *He* was the custodian of the key?'

Posie shrugged. 'Perhaps he was, once. But I think Wykham handed it down. Found a *new* custodian. It even got carried to foreign killing fields, but it found its way home again.'

Lovelace ordered the bunch of keys brought, and opened up the gun cupboard.

The tiny gold key with the angel wings was revealed, hidden behind the awful cap, and if he thought it strange that Posie had found it there, Lovelace didn't say a word about it.

He presented the key on the flat of the palm of his hand to Mr Marchpane, and Regulus didn't lose any time in haring over to the window seat and pressing the golden key this way and that, and then suddenly a clicking noise was heard, and the whole top of the seat disappeared in on itself, on clever runners.

The whole top off, Lovelace peered into the dim cavern down below.

'I can't see a bally thing. Pitch black. It goes a long way down, like a well. Lads, bring me a torch, eh?'

A torch brought, Lovelace shone it and then he glanced up, and gave Posie the briefest of strange stares.

'Right, love, I'm going down. One of you lads follow me, eh? Marchpane, can you telephone to the doctor, right away?'

Posie felt strangely calm. The nausea had gone, and so had the smell.

She remembered Norbert's words: *I'm at the big house in Holt. You know it, I think; Holly House?*

Sounds came from down below. Richard shouting, and the young constable shrieking, and then the sound of the constable being sick.

Lovelace was up again.

He was more ashen than ever Posie had seen him, shaking slightly.

'You were right, darling. Your Reverend is down there, it's all a hell of a state.'

Mr Marchpane looked grey in the face; any vividness gone. 'You're saying my cousin Wykham did this today? Threw poor Carpenter down the hole today?'

Lovelace shook his head. 'Nah. He looks like he's been dead at least two weeks, from what's left of him. I think Wykham must have thrown him down there, from up here, on the day they discovered Peregrine. Carpenter couldn't get out. He'd broken nearly every bone in his body.'

Lovelace turned and helped the constable who was coming up the last rung of the ladder, and he patted the man's back, who was shaking like a jelly.

'Whisky, man. Neat. You'll be right as rain.'

He had a hip-flask in his inner jacket, and he passed it to the constable, who took a good slug before handing it back to Lovelace, who drank it as if it might be water.

Lovelace wiped his mouth with the back of his hand, and gave the hip-flask to Marchpane, who accepted readily, looking like he might pass out.

Lovelace sat down on another window seat. 'There's a gun down there too, probably the one used by old Peregrine Briskow to kill himself. The Webley. It was a smart way for Wykham to get rid of inconvenient evidence quickly. There's a suitcase down there too, looks like it might be full of Carpenter's clothes; maybe Wykham was hoping to make people think the fella had run away?'

'Perhaps.'

Lovelace exhaled. 'One of the worst things I've ever seen, Posie. By Gad. Poor Carpenter must have still been alive when he landed, though; there's a whole heap of firewood thrown down on top of him. I suppose Wykham really had to be *sure* he had killed him. Carpenter died trying to get it off of him; bloodied hands raised up like he was really able to stand a chance of shifting it.'

Posie held onto her husband's shoulder.

She remembered Norbert's mucky hands. She had thought he had been gardening.

She remembered his easy words: *I've been fighting against what felt like an entire forest, and I still show the scars. Sometimes one should recognise one's limits.*

But this had been a man with no limits.

Not even in death.

He was spectacularly unquiet.

What kind of strength had it taken to get to her? To manoeuvre between the interfaces of this world, with its newspapers and bodies, and physical things, and wherever he was now?

He had had one last thing to do, and he had accomplished it.

Girvan was free.

She remembered his words: *I find it almost unbelievable how strong the pull of a heart can be…*

But there was so much Posie didn't understand.

How had he telephoned to her at her office, over and over? How on earth had he managed to get her that sheet of newspaper from *The Norwich Mail* to read? How had there been music played in his rooms, only a couple of days ago? Those types of communication were surely impossible?

Lovelace looked at Posie carefully. 'How on earth did you *know*, my love?'

So far, she hadn't actually told anyone, apart from Girvan, that she had met the Reverend Carpenter in London. She hadn't told a soul about meeting him again last night.

She thought she might keep it that way.

Ghosts are never easy to explain, or laugh off.

Posie shrugged carelessly. 'Norbert Carpenter had to have gone somewhere. And if he'd still been alive, he'd have told the whole world the truth. Wykham *had* to get rid of him; he knew the hidey-holes of this house best of all. Surely it makes sense he would make use of them?'

'Mnnn. But I'm still not clear on one thing. Carpenter looks like he was a tall fella. How on earth did Wykham manoeuvre him down that hole? Surely he'd have put up a bally fight? We know he wasn't shot. There were only two shots heard. He must have been incapacitated in some way.'

Posie nodded. It made an awful sort of sense.

'You're right, I think he *was* incapacitated. When Wykham went to get drinks for both of them in the kitchen, he was already forming a sort of plan. Poor Norbert didn't stand a chance! Norbert was known for his allergies and reactions to things. He nearly died at Christmas when a particularly strong nutmeg was used in the mulled wine. It took him ages to recover. A replacement chaplain even had to be organised. I know Geoffrey had brought a sack of these nutmegs back from India. I believe that Wykham, or his sister, slipped another nutmeg in the glass of red wine which he then drank, unwittingly. I expect Norbert had a bad reaction to it again, some kind of fit; he must have been in a dreadful state. We *know* there was red wine; we saw the residue of it on the desk in the photos.'

'*You* saw it, Posie,' corrected her husband. 'Not Vin.'

But something was puzzling her. 'Wasn't there a dreadful smell down there? Nutmeg? Spices?'

Lovelace pulled Posie to her feet. 'Not at all, love, now you really *are* being fanciful. But I am rather worried by other things which I saw down there, although it might just be a hunch at present. The whole underground tunnel area will need a thorough search. I'll get Dr Poots to oversee Carpenter's autopsy and then his report will tell us everything. I'm going to call him now. Let's get you to the seaside soon, eh? Leave this all for Poots and for the local Forensics team to pick apart. And Vin, who's not quite as bad as I remember, can wrap this all up here. Perhaps Lord Justice Roade will try Wykham? I rather hope so. But I have a feeling he may plead insanity. And I think that fits: the fella must be raving mad.'

Posie shook her head. 'I think he's perfectly in his right mind, darling. This house is a dreadful place. And I don't even know all of its secrets, I'm sure of it.'

* * * *

Epilogue

The winter sun sparkled on the water, far out, at Blakeney Quay.

But it was uncertain weather; a pewter sky promised rain.

The sea air blew over Posie and she was glad she had come back here. But only briefly.

She remembered standing here with her brother after her engagement party, before he had departed for Cambridge. Remembered the hopes and dreams she had had back then.

She was waiting for Lovelace now.

He had immediately gone down into the tunnels again at Holly House, accompanied by Inspector Vin, and they hadn't surfaced for at least an hour.

Since then, he had been cloistered with Vin at the Police Station in Holt. They'd finally emerged, grim-faced, and Lovelace had brought Posie on here.

But he was still busy: right now he was on the telephone again in the lovely Blakeney Hotel which he had booked as a Valentine's treat. He'd needed to make an urgent call to London.

It was after lunch, but Posie had no appetite at all.

They were going to drive a hired car on to Southwold, in Suffolk, which was new for both of them.

No memories, no bodies.

Posie had already been on a walk around Blakeney. She'd seen the church with its sad ship graffiti, and the old Rectory, now changed beyond belief, and she was in a hurry to go.

She sat on a bench with her overnight bag and Lovelace's holdall at her feet, pensive. *More* than pensive.

She had come up against a whole bunch of trouble here. And didn't really want to think it through.

She was suddenly aware of not being alone.

Turning, half in dread, she saw Girvan Briskow was next to her.

She was holding a posy of wintersweet and daffodils. She passed them to Posie, and explained that she'd come on here to Blakeney to clear out Norbert's rooms at the King's Head, which were in a sorry state.

It seemed the Landlady's teenage son, Alfred, had taken to secretly breaking into Norbert's empty rooms with a gang of pals, mainly so they could drink, but Alfred had also been helping himself to Norbert's belongings; even playing records on Norbert's gramophone, which was now broken. Norbert's few records were now all very scratched.

There wasn't much worth salvaging, in fact. Sukey Brown was thoroughly embarrassed, by Alfred's dreadful behaviour, but also for Girvan's wasted trip.

But Girvan had wanted to see Posie, too.

'I knew you were coming on here. I had to follow, to say thank you.'

'Oh.' Posie was touched. 'You're welcome, Mrs Briskow.'

'Call me Girvan, do.'

She felt dreadful for the woman.

Girvan had been told about Norbert's death by Lovelace at the police station in Holt, and apparently she had broken down unconsolably.

'I'm so sorry about Norbert,' Posie said now, not wanting to dodge it all.

Girvan nodded, and sat down heavily next to Posie.

Girvan stared out to sea, calmly. 'I did have half an idea. I kept feeling sick, and smelling again the dreadful scent of his sickness at Christmas. I thought it must be… well, I wondered if I was going mad. So, I held onto hope. And then *you* came. You said Norbert had asked you to come, that you saw him in London.'

Posie was almost run ragged with the strangeness of the case, even in her own mind; it couldn't be explained, not all of it yet, and certainly not to anyone else.

Had she actually imagined the meetings with Norbert Carpenter, after all?

Some strange trick of the mind?

'I'm so sorry for any confusion, Girvan. I genuinely *did* think I had met with your fiancé.'

'Well, whatever has happened here, thank heavens you came.'

The tiny dark girl wiped her eyes brusquely. 'You must have thought us very rude, at Holly House. All those years ago.'

Posie frowned. 'Well, you were consistent with it, so I accepted it, I suppose. I didn't understand the hatred, though. In fact, the first time I met you I heard you telling one of your sisters-in-law that I was the devil. What was the problem with me?'

Girvan almost laughed. 'I *wondered* if you had heard that, Miss Parker. You got the wrong end of the stick. Or rather just the end of a saying. I think I was saying we should "Tell the truth and shame the devil." *Not* that you were the devil. No: not at all.'

'So, what was going on?'

Girvan was wearing a warm black cap and a big muffler, sensible for here.

She burrowed down into it. 'I should explain. There's only *me* left to explain, and I'm leaving soon. It's about Harry, of course.'

'Oh? Not about me? I thought you all hated *me*?'

'We adored you. Old Peregrine more than anyone. He was a big softie. He could see how young and beautiful and perfect you were. A rare girl. A perfect wife for a Briskow son. He didn't know what to do. He told us to put you off; thought that if we were all rude enough you might change your mind about Harry, and leave him. But you were insistent, weren't you? You clung on. You were *far* too good for him. And he was far too bad for you.'

Posie stared at Girvan, a girl who could have been her sister-in-law, if fates had allowed.

'*Harry?* Bad? Are we talking about the same boy here? My Harry?'

Girvan laughed bitterly. 'Your sweet, mild, bespectacled Harry?'

Posie nodded.

And then came a tale of darkness.

Utter shame.

A boy adored by his mother, who could do no wrong, who was spoilt rotten.

A boy who got everything he wanted. A boy who liked to light fires, and who set up a small chemistry lab in an attic room of the house. A boy who liked to take photographs, and whose mother bought him all the equipment, even setting up a dark room for him.

An inexplicable accident when he was twelve, with chemicals, with his mother within that locked dark room had ended in tragedy, with Emily Briskow dead.

An accident which was hushed up, and moved on from.

Years of mess and trouble.

Changes of school, and expulsions. Reports of violence, bullying.

One lad had been left paralysed by Harry, who had beaten him with a cricket bat until he was left senseless. Peregrine had paid the family off; it was all hushed up.

There were dreadful endless school holidays when

Harry would roam the woods around Holt hunting for animals.

Experiments, torture.

Then a peaceful year or two when Harry had been sent away to a hospital in Scotland.

Girvan had married Joseph by this point, and she heard all about Harry. The black sheep of the family.

A devil of a boy.

She felt the relief of the family when Harry had returned to Norfolk and had seemed calm, quiet; dulled perhaps by drugs?

He'd expressed an interest in law and it was all arranged with that nice Marchpane solicitor who was paid a handsome stipend to take Harry on, knowing all about his previous background.

But Harry had done surprisingly well there, and to the world it was as if Harry had turned over a new leaf. He cycled, and he had a motor car, and he played cricket.

Posie swallowed.

She whispered fearfully: 'But he *hadn't* turned over a new leaf? He was still the same?'

Girvan Briskow shook her head: 'No. Not the same. Worse. He turned away from animals, and he sought out women. *Everywhere.* In the cinema, and in the woods, in the house, and in the brothels. He was very clever about it; so mild on the outside and with the nice car for giving these girls a ride in. But there was a time when no girl in service would come and work at Holly House. The ones who did arrive would end up pregnant, crying, worse. There was always a snivelling girl with a story to tell. In fact, *do* you remember Millie? You said you did, today?'

Posie nodded, hardly wanting to hear more, sick in her heart, which juddered horribly.

'The day Harry invited you for tea that first time, it was only ten minutes or so after we had all found out that Millie was pregnant, by Harry. Millie had told Sir Peregrine, and then Sir Peregrine called a house meeting, without servants. Millie had trusted Sir Peregrine, hoped he'd fix things for her with Harry; she aimed high. Harry couldn't have cared less: wouldn't even look over at Millie at that tea, and she had been convinced that he was going to marry her! Joe, my husband, bless his soul, was incandescent with rage at Harry. But he and I, we said we would help Millie: take her to a Nursing Home to have the child, but she insisted on the other route. And I'm afraid it wasn't a happy one for her... So, you can see you rather walked in on a nightmare that day. Not that it was your fault. But we didn't want *that* fate to befall you.'

Posie felt dead inside, licked her lips. 'Why didn't you just *tell* me?'

'I think I wanted to, and hence my trying to insist to name Harry as a 'devil'. But would you have listened? We could see you were dogged. And headstrong. Perhaps that's why Harry didn't hurt you? You were different to all the others, and also, you were genuinely beautiful, classy. Wife material. Worth looking after. Maybe like a precious object? We all prayed that Harry would be called up first in the Great War. That the problem would go away. It sounds awful but we all hoped he would die. He did, but quite late in the day... And not before other terrible things happened.'

Posie stared. She was remembering her father's doubts; how he'd claimed Harry was 'wrong'.

Had her father meant wrong for *her*, or generally a 'wrong' sort of person?

Had he sensed the danger Posie was facing?

Had her brother also realised?

These warnings had been unwanted, and she'd ignored them. At her peril, it now seemed.

Girvan was chattering away, as if desperate to get things off her chest.

'There were two dreadful crimes which took place in

1917, but they were hushed up. Girls going missing. Low-class girls; not loved and hence not missed. Sheringham and Cromer girls. These disappearances both coincided with Harry's leave in April. I don't know if you recall, he was only back briefly?'

'Mnnn. He was perfectly pleasant to me, but he was jittery, on edge. I put it all down to the Great War, of course.'

'The girls were found dead, battered; attacked with a cricket bat. There was never any direct evidence, but we, the family, *knew*. It had happened once before, you see, back in 1914. There had been several prostitutes being attacked back then, all in a cluster; dumped in pinewoods or wasteland, their skulls cracked like eggs. Sir Peregrine found Harry's cricket bat in the back of his Ford, covered in hair and blood, and Harry shrugged it off, almost laughed about it. The stories never made the papers, although I tried to find out as much as possible about the girls who had died, and get involved in trying to make a difference to the lives of the friends they had left behind; trying to offer some practical and monetary support. Sir Peregrine was right behind me every step, even back then.'

Posie's thoughts were racing, remembering her own brother's warning about a story he had heard on a train. A hushed-up tale of caution, a poor girl who had come to harm.

She remembered Harry's words across the years: *A straight bat, but wielded strongly.*

His long fingers, calloused underneath from the bat.

She thought she might be sick.

Girvan carried on in a much lower voice. 'Sir Peregrine was beside himself: the only power he had over Harry was money, and he withheld a marriage settlement from him again and again. He also encouraged him to join up, again and again.'

Girvan stared at the sea hard. 'He feared his own son,

you see. Although I think he even had doubts sometimes as to whether Harry was *his* son. I think he thought Harry might be Wykham's son. Wykham certainly took a lot of interest in Harry, and he was his favourite of the boys. Although Harry wouldn't have wanted to be anything other than a Briskow. He was very proud of being a Briskow.'

Posie remembered the angel wing key necklace, and the idea of passing it on from one generation of the Marchpane family to the next.

If Harry *had* been Wykham's natural son then he was the obvious recipient for the gift, and the fact Harry had it at all made sense.

But this custodian had not been an angel.

Not at all.

Posie felt sick.

Was this all true? Could she really believe that mild Harry, who had only ever been gentleness itself, and whom, in her naïve way she had trusted, was capable of such horrors?

Had he really been capable of such cruelty?

Had she really, voluntarily, placed herself for the taking in such a man's path? Body and soul? And why had he treated her so well, and so nicely, if he treated other women so badly?

Had it all just been an act? How long could it have lasted before she had come to harm, and he'd slipped?

She remembered the hazy summer days: the cycle rides, the gifts, the outings.

The mauve beach hut.

Harry's skin; the golden necklace against his skin.

He had never shown a single second of brutality. Although there had been that odd blankness, that gulf of understanding. Which Posie had tried to gloss over at the time as being not insurmountable.

Girvan stood up, patted down her coat.

'Peregrine never recovered from Harry, not really. He

felt Harry was a curse on the family, and that he, Peregrine, had somehow been at fault. Even when Harry was dead he nagged at Peregrine; Peregrine couldn't escape the horror. I suppose that's why he used Harry's pistol, in the end. There were never any pictures up of Harry, either. Peregrine couldn't bear to see them. And he wanted desperately to 'make up' for what Harry had done to those women, you see. That's why the Briskow money goes for projects to help others just like them. Anyway, I'm glad you survived it all.'

'Me too.'

Posie thought of the solicitor, Marchpane, who had worked with Harry. *Had he known about the women?* He had always seemed reluctant to discuss Harry with her; saying openly that he had never wanted Harry as a long-term partner.

What was it he had said to Posie yesterday?

Devils have had angels' faces before, Miss Parker.

But you know that, of course.

Had Marchpane known the extent of the evil involved? He had certainly known *something*.

Posie stood up with the posy of flowers propped in her arms.

'What will you do now, Mrs Briskow?'

'I'm leaving, of course. I'm booked on a passage to America with Geoffrey. New York. We'll travel as husband and wife; we share the same surname, so it should be easy. And I'm pregnant, I expect you knew that, though. So it will make it easier if my child, Norbert's child, has a father.'

Posie had half-suspected.

'You'll use the Briskow money, when everything here is sold?'

'I will. There are plenty of destitute teenage girls in America, I expect. The big cities. Peregrine didn't limit me with a place, or a country. Perhaps I can do some good over there for a while.'

Girvan was scrabbling in one of her big coat pockets.

'Here we are! Your earrings. I'm sorry I was mean when you first turned up wearing them; they're delightful, and fancy, and made by Cartier! And they *were* very lucky for me. I think it was also your message, about them being lucky, delivered by Inspector Vin, that made me think I might really have a chance of getting out of all this mess alive. Thank you.'

She passed them across and Posie tucked them away, for the next time.

'I'm certain that you can do wonderful things in America, Girvan. Good luck with your baby. Norbert would have been so excited.'

'You too, with yours. You're pregnant too, aren't you? Come on, I can tell: I'm a midwife!'

But just at this moment Lovelace arrived, pulling his hands through his thick red hair, looking distracted. He caught sight of the two women, and he brandished an umbrella for them.

'Rain is coming,' he said cheerfully. 'The barometer in the hotel there was going back. Are you two taking a walk?'

'No. I must be off,' said Girvan quickly. 'Geoffrey and I are collecting a dog he'd bought a couple of weeks ago. He was going to keep it at Holly House, only Norbert was allergic to it, so he boarded it out almost immediately. It was only at Holly House an hour or so when Norbert started scratching. We'll collect it now, take it to America with us.'

Posie frowned. 'Is it a black dog?'

Girvan nodded. 'That's right. A Labrador.'

Posie pressed on, insistent. 'Did everyone see it, at Holly House? For this one hour? Sir Peregrine?'

'Oh, probably not. I think Sir Peregrine was sleeping on and off in his study at the time. Geoffrey put the dog in the green parlour for a bit. I doubt Peregrine saw it, not even for a few seconds.'

Oh, but he did, Posie thought to herself.

He did. He must have wandered in…

Posie felt like she was standing on slightly firmer ground for a second or so.

And then Girvan waved, and walked away.

* * * *

'Darling, come inside for a bit,' Lovelace said, after Girvan left. 'There's someone inside who wants to chat.'

'Oh?'

Posie and he walked into the beautiful Blakeney Hotel where the tiles were polished and the wood was gleaming and the mirrors reflected cosy glamour.

Over in a huge armchair by the fire, smoking a cigar, was Rufus, Eleventh Earl of Cardigeon.

On one side of him tucked in tight was a glamorous young blonde in an emerald silk dress, the kind of slip you might wear for evening, and on the other side was a gorgeous young man, dark with curly hair and the sort of caramel-toffee-coloured eyes you could get lost in for days.

The young man was drinking a tiny glass of milk and soda.

'I need to make one more telephone call, then we'll leave,' said Lovelace certainly, and Posie headed towards Rufus while Lovelace stayed up at the bar.

Rufus, as was his wont, had drunk a good deal, neat whisky mainly, despite the fact it was early. His blue eyes were blazing, and his face glowed an unhealthy red.

It was quite a remove from the handsome blonde boy of seventeen who had played cricket on the sands here and tagged along for whole summers of fresh air.

'Rufus?'

'Wotcha, Nosey,' said Rufus happily, inhaling some cigar smoke and blowing a perfect smoke ring.

'I was wondering when you'd turn up here. I thought you were getting a bit high and mighty for your old pal Rufus, eh? Not bothering to return my messages.'

Posie sat down quickly, and took the milk and soda which the waiter offered.

'What messages, Rufey? I don't think I've got a single one. Mind you, I *have* got the worst secretary in the world right now. It's possible she's overlooked them, or eaten them or something,'

Rufus snorted with derision. 'Yes, I've spoken to her. She seems not quite the ticket, what? I kept calling, actually. Again and again: she always says "Is it you again, sir?" I *did* give my name but I haven't the foggiest if she wrote it down, eh? I wanted you to come up here pronto, Posie: I've taken up semi-permanent residence here with Gina here, and Diego.'

A look of fondness spread across his face.

'I always remember our days here in Blakeney: some of the happiest in my life. I wanted to recreate that, and kill some time over winter. Thought you might be enticed up here, too? I even found a juicy page of local gossip involving a murder case! Some place called 'Holt'! Did you see it? I ripped the sheet out and sent it down to you? Thought it might whet your appetite and you'd come roaring up here. I see it worked!'

Posie sipped at her drink slowly.

So it had been Rufus who had been Suzannah's annoying male caller, ringing on and on.

And it had been Rufus who had sent the piece from *The Norwich Mail.*

Not Norbert Carpenter.

Both things had been completely explicable. As had the playing of the music in Norbert's rooms.

She sighed.

Well, good job.

There was something else which had been bothering

Posie only the day before and she raised it now with her old friend. Tried to keep the resentment out of her voice completely.

'I was thinking about that time too, Rufus, when you boys went up to Cambridge. I was left here alone, and I needed a job. I asked *you* to supply me with a reference. I wanted a job at New Scotland Yard. I don't suppose you recall this?'

Rufus ground out his cigar in the glass ashtray and frowned.

'Of course I do, Nosey. I bally well spent an age writing you that reference. And what's more, I saw you needed *two*. I went specially to post a request to old Morrissey, you remember him? Our summertime tutor, up from Eton? He of the floppy hair? He quite liked you, as it happens. He wrote you a reference too, and I packaged them up together and I was going to send them both to you when your brother Richard came into my rooms and said he'd be up here in Blakeney again in two shakes of a lamb's tail; he'd bring the packet up to you.'

Posie stared. '*And*? What happened next?'

Rufus blustered. 'I don't know, old girl. I presumed you didn't get the job, eh? I never heard about it ever again, until now. Are you telling me that your brother *never* delivered them to you?'

It didn't do to speak ill of the dead, but it didn't do to dress things up in finery either.

Richard Parker, Posie's brother, had had some failings. Forgetfulness had been one, and giving in to their father had been another.

The two references had either been lost, or confiscated. On purpose or by accident. Blown by fate on a wind which had passed Posie right by.

There was no use in trying to decipher it now.

'Thank you, Rufey,' she said, standing up. 'I *do* appreciate the effort you went to.'

She saw that Lovelace had finished his call and was at the bar still, scratching through some notes in his pocketbook.

'I loved your brother more than life itself,' said Rufus suddenly.

'But he was an unreliable so-and-so. Like that one time when I asked him whether he thought I should marry you: just before the Great War? He said he'd write to you about it on a postcard, and then let me have your reply. But no answer ever came. In the end I gave up and went off to the war unmarried. Hey-ho. I suppose, hearing your tale just now, that he probably never sent you a postcard, did he? Just japed about?'

Posie narrowed her eyes.

What on earth had her brother been playing at? What had been his aim in all of this misdirection?

Perhaps she would never find out.

'Did you really want to marry me, Rufey?' she asked, her voice slightly softer now.

'Well… I suppose I thought we'd rub along well enough together, and that you wouldn't mind my shenanigans.'

She looked across to Gina, and Diego, who were fawning for Rufus' attention; Diego in particular was very close to Rufus. And Posie remembered her brother saying Rufus would be suitable for her in temperament, but that she couldn't marry Rufus.

She'd got angry. Thought he'd meant she wasn't good enough.

But it seemed to be something else which ran deeper.

How had Posie never noticed it until now? But there was always a string of gorgeous young people about Rufus. Gorgeous girls, and many gorgeous boys.

Had it been because of all this extra circus on the side?

Had her brother known, all along? Had he even been part of it, at some point?

And what had Dolly, when married to Rufus, made of it all?

The shenanigans.

At the bar, Lovelace was drinking neat whisky with no water or ice. It was a bad sign in his case. Posie went over and climbed up on the stool next to him, clinked her glass against his.

He smiled, but there was pain there.

'Richard? I was just speaking to Rufus, darling. Years ago, I decided I wanted to work at Scotland Yard, and I asked him to be my reference. We were just reminiscing.'

Lovelace frowned. 'Scotland Yard?'

'Mnnn. They were advertising for ten lady police officers.'

Lovelace swallowed, almost choked. 'By Gad, I recall. Did you apply?'

'Not in the end. No.'

His face broke into an easy smile. 'Thank Goodness. I thought I might have passed you by, which would have been bally awful! I was one of the selection committee, you see. Hundreds of women applied. We had a hard job rootling out the best, and most had faked their own references. It's how I met my wife, Molly. She was one of the ten successful girls. She loved it at first, but had to pack it in when Phyllis was born. It was jolly hard work, too. Dangerous in the City and East End. Some of the girls got attacked: two of them died on the job. It was decided to phase the whole thing out.'

Posie nodded.

It seemed right that Molly Lovelace had been a police officer. She had sounded sensible and hard-working and very, very unafraid.

Someone I would have been friends with, Posie thought to herself in surprise.

'Posie,' said Lovelace, and he sounded very serious, 'I have been around the tunnels of Holly House and they are now being investigated properly, with a big team coming up from London, but I wanted you to know that there is something there, at Holly House, which directly concerns you.'

What doesn't concern me, there?

Posie met her husband's green eyes and locked onto their constant and steady gaze.

'Go on,' she whispered.

'It seems that there was a young lad, his name was Harry Briskow. He had the only access down into those tunnels, and out again, into remote pinewoods and scrubland. Wykham has confirmed it. That carved angel-wing key was Harry's. Wykham gave it to him when the lad was eighteen, and Wykham drew him a map of the tunnels. A kind of 'present' it seems. A place he could run riot.'

'Mnnn?'

Posie's heart was pounding. *What on earth was Lovelace about to tell her?*

'When we were investigating, Vin and I found two very old skeletons, probably as old as the house itself: a human and a dog. Likely they got trapped.'

Posie nodded. 'That must be the civil war priest, and his dog. You've found them, then. An old legend made real.'

Lovelace squeezed her hand. 'Can you be brave, my love?'

'I'm always brave.'

'I know.'

He swallowed. 'I think that this lad Harry may have been a serial killer, darling. Those tunnels were both a playground and a hiding-place for his crimes. There were other bodies down in the tunnels, too. Quite a few. All women. I'd say they date from the last fifteen years. I've been on the telephone to Norwich: asking for missing persons files for Norfolk. These lasses were all murdered with the heads bashed in. Bad killings, love.'

Posie shivered.

'Darling, one of the girls was known to *you*.'

Posie had started to tremble, panic filling the place where her lungs should be. 'Who is she?'

'I don't know her name, my love. But she was holding a small present, wrapped up for you. It had your name - 'POSIE PARKER- UNTIL WE MEET AGAIN!' - on top, and inside was a silver notebook and a silver pencil. And what looks like a lipstick. I've had to leave the present for the Forensics team to date and file.'

Posie must have been looking blank, and Lovelace pulled something out from his pocketbook.

It was tiny.

Cream, and green and violet. That small slogan VOTES FOR WOMEN! was emblazoned along the top.

Posie took the pin and then her tears came unbidden.

Lovelace spoke softly. 'She had black hair, my love, this lass: and a brand-new nurses' kit in her satchel. It was all intact, never yet worn.'

Hattie.

Dear Hattie, who hadn't just left without saying goodbye.

Who hadn't died out in France, as everyone had supposed.

Posie remembered her small engagement party at her father's Rectory; the way Hattie had been laughing along with Harry, and then how she had moved off to speak to Girvan.

Had Harry felt slighted?

Or had he wanted poor Hattie in a way she wouldn't give in to?

Brave, bold Hattie.

What fierce and terrible madness had driven Harry? Why had she, Posie, been allowed to live?

Perhaps to be here, now.

'I need to leave,' Posie said firmly. She wanted to leave all these ghosts behind.

'Good, our hired car is around the front. All ready.'

Posie and Lovelace walked out quickly and stood beside the water, and the sky was a thousand colours of purple, sultry as a bruise.

Her brother's words came to her again. Clear as a bell this time. As if he were here right now.

Time is precious: don't fill it up with nonsense.

Richard Parker had been a brother who had sometimes acted oddly, infuriatingly, but who had ultimately protected Posie in the long-run.

She wished suddenly that he could have met Lovelace.

'Richard, meet Richard.'

There was nothing drippy about Lovelace. Her brother would have seen that. And Lovelace understood Posie in a way few other men could.

She'd better forget this nonsense with the girl down in London. Had better hope it was a phase.

'Darling,' she said, as Lovelace was busy packing the holdalls into the back of the hired car, 'You'll need to take that nice gold Valentine's ring back to the Burlington Arcade when we get back to London.'

'What?'

He screwed his eyes up in confusion. 'But you told me you liked it?'

She watched the sails on the boats whip in the wind, and Posie saw the fishermen folding their nets away for the day.

'I *do*. But it's not yet complete.'

'You mean…?'

'Yes. I'm pretty certain.'

And Lovelace threw back his head and laughed joyfully and took Posie into his arms.

'Oh, sweetheart…'

But just at this moment the sky split with lightning, and the clouds moved apart over the grey, grey sea.

'I love a storm,' said Posie, smiling.

'I know that, darling,' said Lovelace, kissing her cheek. 'I always think that if there was a perfect perfume for you, it would be a storm in a bottle. You'd try and capture the weather as it changes. The scent of danger, perhaps.'

Posie held onto Lovelace's hand and she gripped him tight.

In that moment she felt as if she would never let him go.

****

Thank you for joining Posie Parker

Enjoyed *Murder and the Scent of Nutmeg* (A Posie Parker Mystery #16)? Here's what you can do next.

If you could take a moment to leave a short review on the platform where you purchased the book, it would be immensely helpful.

Your reviews play a significant role in spreading the word about the series and assisting new readers in discovering it.

In addition to "Murder and the Scent of Nutmeg", Posie's other intriguing cases are available in various formats to suit your preference. You can find all the books, listed in chronological order here: https://www.amazon.com/author/lbhathaway

They are available in e-book and paperback formats, as well as in Audiobook format for those who prefer to listen.

Don't miss out! Take a moment to follow on Amazon and/or subscribe to the newsletter:

1. **Follow on Amazon:** Visit www.amazon.com/author/lbhathaway and click on "+Follow" button.

2. **Subscribe to the Newsletter:** Simply visit www.lbhathaway.com and enter your email address in the subscription box. By subscribing, you'll receive exclusive content, behind-the-scenes insights, and special offers straight to your inbox.

Historical Note

All of the characters in this novel are fictional, unless specifically mentioned below. Weather, timings, general political events, and places (and descriptions of places) are historically accurate to the best of my knowledge, save for any exceptions listed below.

As in the other Posie Parker books, I refer to the First World War of 1914–1918 as the 'Great War' throughout, which is simpler for the modern reader, although it would not have been referred to in this way in 1926.

As ever, Posie's work address in London (Grape Street, Bloomsbury, WC1) and her home address around the corner (Museum Chambers, WC1) are both very real, although you might have to do a bit of imagining to find her there.

1. (Throughout) For the Temple Church, please see: www.templechurch.com. The church is a real treat to visit, both at Christmas and other times of the year. Please note that the painted medieval interior of the dome as described in this novel is now different (the walls are now plain tempered white). This and other changes in the church were mainly caused by the direct bomb which was dropped on the Temple Church in

WW2 (1941) and the catastrophic damage suffered as a result, both to the dome and the main nave, or 'chancel'. Although lovingly restored, the church took years to repair.

2. (Chapter Two) The church which Posie's father is (fictitiously) the Rector of is the real-life church of St Nicholas at Blakeney, in Norfolk, one of five churches in the Glaven Valley Benefice, within the Diocese of Norwich. This beautiful coastal thirteenth-century church with its famous two towers is well worth an explore, especially to see the mediaeval graffiti featuring boats. Please note that the disorganisation of the Reverend Parker's own professional life, and his sickness and his personality, is entirely a fiction of my own and he is not based on any real-life person. For the church itself see: https://glavenvalleychurches.org.uk

3. (Chapter Two) For the mystery of the disappearance of Posie's mother, Rosa, and for more Parker family secrets, see *A Christmas Case* (a standalone Posie Parker Novella) and also *Murder and the Mermaid: A Posie Parker Mystery #13*.

4. (Chapter Two) There was indeed a shop and Post Office run by a Mr Joshua Parker in Blakeney during this time, on the High Street. The proposed Hotel for tourists which is referred to here in this novel as an aspiration in 1913 was eventually built in 1921. It started trading in 1923 and this beautiful water-front hotel is still going strong today. See: https://www.blakeney-hotel.co.uk

5. (Chapter Two) The shops in Holt are accurate as to the date of this novel, but the Sunbeam bicycle in the window of Neal's is a fancy of my own (although

the model of the bicycle itself was real). The silver notebooks and the stationery on display in the window of F. W. Baker are also fictional. Please note that although the silver notebooks are fictional, these remain a common motif and are used by Posie throughout this series.

6. (Chapter Two) Mrs Pankhurst's Suffragettes, the 'WSPU' (Women's Social and Political Union) had an office on 52, London Street, Norwich, from 1912 onwards, organising a big march in the city in 1913, demonstrating against the deplorable 'Cat and Mouse Act' which enabled the force-feeding of suffragette prisoners while in jail. However, as stated in this novel, Norwich was not as forward about women's suffrage in ways that other cities were; nor was Norwich's WSPU group as militant as other groups. This is, as noted here in this story, in direct contrast to their neighbouring WSPU group in Great Yarmouth, who really did burn down the town pier in an act of purposeful violence in 1913.

7. Peregrine Briskow and his family (throughout) are all completely fictional, as is Holly House in Holt. The solicitors' firm of Marchpane & Marchpane is also fictional. However, the Department Store in Holt, with the nice restaurant where Posie meets Harry for the first time, is real. It is Bakers & Larners. See: https://www.bakersandlarners.co.uk/

8. (Chapter Three) There were bombing raids in the Great War, including Zeppelin or 'flying bomb' attacks and raids. The bombs falling over the Norfolk coast in January 1915 were essentially a result of the German bombing crews having flown off course; they were meaning to attack Hull and the Humber estuary.

9. (Chapter Four) As with the reference to Millie, the Briskow's Parlourmaid, the chemicals (TNT, in particular, used to fill shells and grenades) used by female munitions workers in the Great War would often turn their skin and hair bright yellow, cause liver problems, reproductive health-related problems and a whole range of other (sometimes fatal) side-effects. These girls were known as 'Canary Girls.'

10. (Throughout) George Thalben-Ball was the real-life resident choirmaster, composer, director and organist at the Temple Church, from 1923 to 1982. He was famous in his lifetime and is known mainly for the Temple Church Choir's very famous performance and recording in 1927 of Mendelssohn's 'Hear My Prayer'. I have played with the timing here and placed that recording (on the HMV label) in 1926 rather than 1927, so Norbert Carpenter can say he owns it and enjoys listening to it.

11. (Chapter Four) *The Norwich Mail* is fictional, as is the story of the death about which Posie reads.

12. (Chapter Four) The door I describe next to the effigies of the Knights is fictional, although, as detailed at point 1 above, the interior of the Temple Church is now different from its 1926 incarnation.

13. (Chapter Five) My version of Holt Police Station and those working in it is entirely fictional. The Feathers Hotel on the Market Square (where Posie stays) was and is real, although the view from her room of Holly House (fictional) and the Police Station (also fictional) is obviously made up. (See: https://www.thefeathersholt.com)

14. (Chapter Six) The coach crash which fictionally kills Kate Briskow and her daughters is the real-life crash of June 1925, when the York to Grassington coach overturned into a ravine killing 7 people and maiming another 14.

* * * *

About the Author

Cambridge-educated, British-born L.B. Hathaway writes historical fiction. She worked as a lawyer at Lincoln's Inn in London for almost a decade before becoming a full-time writer. She is a lifelong fan of detective novels set in the Golden Age of Crime.

Her other interests, in no particular order, are: very fast downhill skiing, theatre-going, drinking strong tea, Tudor history, exploring castles and generally trying to cram as much into life as possible.

The Posie Parker series of cosy crime novels span the 1920s. They each combine a core central mystery, an exploration of the reckless glamour of the age and a feisty protagonist who you would love to have as your best friend.

Get in touch with L.B. Hathaway or follow her on social media:

author@lbhathaway.com

Newsletter sign up:
https://www.lbhathaway.com

Goodreads:
https://www.goodreads.com/lbhathaway

Facebook:
https://m.facebook.com/L-B-Hathaway-books-1423516601228019/

Instagram:
https://www.instagram.com/l.b.hathaway_author

Twitter:
https://twitter.com/LbHathaway

Printed in Great Britain
by Amazon

49207772R00103